JOHN BUCHAN led a [...] diplomat, soldier, barrister, jou[...], [...], politician, publisher, poet and novelist. He was born in Perth in 1875, the eldest son of a Free Church of Scotland minister, and educated at Hutcheson's Grammar School in Glasgow. He graduated from Glasgow University then took a scholarship to Oxford. During his time there – 'spent peacefully in an enclave like a monastery' – he wrote two historical novels.

In 1901 he became a barrister of the Middle Temple and a private secretary to the High Commissioner for South Africa. In 1907 he married Susan Charlotte Grosvenor; they had three sons and a daughter. After spells as a war correspondent, Lloyd George's Director of Information and a Conservative MP, Buchan moved to Canada in 1935 where he became the first Baron Tweedsmuir of Elsfield.

Despite poor health throughout his life, Buchan's literary output was remarkable – thirty novels, over sixty non-fiction books, including biographies of Sir Walter Scott and Oliver Cromwell, and seven collections of short stories. His distinctive thrillers – 'shockers' as he called them – were characterised by suspenseful atmosphere, conspiracy theories and romantic heroes, notably Richard Hannay (based on the real-life military spy William Ironside) and Sir Edward Leithen. Buchan was a favourite writer of Alfred Hitchcock, whose screen adaptation of *The Thirty-Nine Steps* was phenomenally successful.

John Buchan served as Governor-General of Canada from 1935 until his death in 1940, the year his autobiography *Memory Hold-the-door* was published.

STELLA RIMINGTON spent her career in MI5, working in counter-espionage, counter-subversion and counter-terrorism, becoming Director-General from 1992 to 1996. Her autobiography *Open Secret* was published in 2001 and since then she has written several thrillers, all broadly based on her experiences and featuring MI5 officer Liz Carlyle.

JOHN BUCHAN

The Power-House

Introduced by Stella Rimington

First published in 1913 by *Blackwood's Magazine*.
This edition published in Great Britain in 2018 by Polygon,
an imprint of Birlinn Ltd.

West Newington House
10 Newington Road
Edinburgh
EH9 1QS

www.polygonbooks.co.uk

3

ISBN 978 1 84697 029 0

British Library Cataloguing-in-Publication Data
A catalogue record for this book is available
on request from the British Library.

Printed and bound in Great Britain
by Clays Ltd, Elcograf S.p.A.

Contents

Contents

Introduction

The Power-House is one of the least known of Buchan's
mature works, a tale without a plot, and so full of holes that
it calls to mind Samuel Johnson's definition of a 'network' –
'anything reticulated and desuccated, at equal distances, with
interstices between the intersections'. It is pure essence of
Buchan – a demonstration of his magical power to weave a
tale out of no materials but the threads and colours of his
imagination. It does, however, possess a theme – John
Bunyan's idea, in *Pilgrim's Progress*, of men of goodwill and
courage struggling with an intelligent, evil power at the root of
all the world's troubles and confusions. The same idea
inspired the Richard Hannay stories that quickly followed
the appearance of *The Power-House* in 1913: *The Thirty-nine
Steps*, *Greenmantle*, *Mr Standfast* and *The Three Hostages*.
However, in none of Buchan's books is there a keener sense
of place or a clearer victory of sense over unreason than in *The
Power-House*.

The novel was written for *Blackwood's Magazine* at a time
when Buchan, working with the Scottish publisher Nelson,
was bringing out pocket editions of literature. Already a best-
selling novelist – *Prester John* was published in 1910 – the back
of his mind must have been full of scraps of A.E.W. Mason,
W.W. Jacobs, H.G. Wells, Conrad and Hilaire Belloc, all
republished at sevenpence, as well as ideas from his long-

time favourites, Stevenson, Kipling, Conan Doyle, Rider Haggard and possibly even from Edgar Wallace, whose *Four Just Men* came out in 1906. Strains of all these permeate *The Power-House*. It needed only the advent of the Great War, together with a powerful injection of Buchan's own international wartime intelligence experiences and a string of characters drawn from his wide circle of political and military friends, to turn *The Power-House* formula into that of the Hannay books.

In his autobiography, published in 1940, Buchan confesses he is 'fascinated by the notion of hurried journeys . . . a theme common to Homer and the penny reciters, [appealing] to a very ancient instinct in human nature . . . Whether failure or success results, life is sharpened, intensified, idealised'. *The Power-House* embodies this philosophy, as well as Buchan's conception of the hero as a man of sense, the best of his land and country, a thoroughgoing Eton-educated gentleman. Such a man is intelligent enough not to be 'brainy', and is most fully alive when, abandoning comfort, he confronts the wild – conceived of as a moor or mountain inhabited by hostile foreigners.

The hero of *The Power-House* is Leithen (named after a tributary of the River Tweed in Scotland). Like Buchan, he is a barrister, but also a sportsman. Buchan sets his protagonist the task of solving the problems of a lady troubled with a disappearing husband. However, it is a smoking-room desperado who goes to Uzbekistan to do the actual husband-rescuing rough stuff, while Leithen is subjected to the attentions of the Evil One in the streets of London and the leafy byways of Surrey. The storytelling touch, which never fails with Buchan, is to mirror the cheerful and the humdrum with the deeply sinister and the threatening, producing a kind of nightmare which only steadfast courage and good judgement can restore to sanity and sense.

However, Leithen's virtues are hardly the point of interest. What really makes this book hum is the first appearance of the Buchan villain, already fully fledged. In this tale he is called Andrew Lumley, but in later books much the same character appears as Graf von Schwabing, Medina or even Hilda von Einem. Lumley, alias Julius Pavia, is English, but with a touch of the Hapsburg about his jaw. Like von Schwabing in *The Thirty-nine Steps*, Buchan makes him appear first in a library. Medina in *The Three Hostages* also has a library – 'as mysterious as the aisles of a forest', filled with 'books, books, old books full of forgotten knowledge'.

Curiously, all the Buchan villains have sinister eyes, Lumley so much so that he has to wear green spectacles. Von Schwabing can hood his eyes like a hawk and they are, moreover, 'cold, malignant, unearthly and horribly clever'. Medina's are 'not the pale blue . . . [of] our Norse ancestry, but [like] a sapphire, entrancing'. Von Einem's eyes pass the paleness test, but are 'strange, potent . . . the cold eyes of the fanatic'. However, she has compensatory aspects.

Despite their menacing eyes, alien names and jawlines, Buchan's villains, like his heroes, move in the best circles and attend the most distinguished dinners. They play for the highest stakes. But their sophistication is a masquerade – middle-classness lurks not far beneath the surface. Lumley has mercantile connections, a house in Blackheath, and a very un-Jeeves-like ex-trades-unionist butler. Von Schwabing looks like Mr Pickwick, calls himself 'Moxon Ivery', addresses a meeting of the 'New Movement' in Biggleswick and plays tennis under the pseudonym of Percy Appleton. No gentleman would dream of doing any of that. Even Medina, though indubitably a squire, performs evil deeds in Gospel Oak.

Furthermore, they are all spies and impersonators. Granted, Hannay is not averse to amateur dramatics, but despite passing for a renegade Dutch peasant or a Highland road-mender, he remains ineffably gentlemanly. At no time does Hannay resort to hypnosis to learn the enemy's secrets, as Medina does, or size them up for seduction like von Einem, or seek, like Lumley, to undermine their morale with tall propositions about the twilight of the world.

It is never clear in Buchan's tales what really drives all these villains on. What are they actually after? When Leithen ventures to probe this, Lumley answers, 'How should I be able to tell you? . . . I cannot pry into motives . . . I only know of the existence of vast extra-social intelligences; let us say that they distrust the machine.' According to MacGillivray of Scotland Yard, more clues are available 'in the sonnet of a poet anarchist who shot himself in the slums of Antwerp, and in the extra-ordinary testimony of a Professor M— of Jena who at the age of thirty-seven took his life after writing a strange mystical message to his fellow-citizens.' Tantalising stuff, but we learn no more.

In Buchan, the fate of the villains does not vary – defeated by straight dealing and gentlemanly behaviour, they simply deliquesce. Schwabing does so twice, once during a bombing raid on London and then again when made to fight honestly, at which point he runs and is shot by his own people. Medina, cornered on a crag, unsportingly attempts a murder and falls to his death, but it is left uncertain as to whether this is through suicide or fatigue. Lumley does at least meet the final act like a gentleman. He tries a bargain, recognises defeat, and promptly expires. One thing is clear: vanity and ambition does for all of them. Von Einem is the exception – she fails, of course, because she is a woman. Her sin is pride, not vanity, and she dies like a hero.

Of course, the Buchan villain never operates single-handedly: behind each one can be found armies of underlings. At least three hundred aides, many in disguise, must have been required to track Leithen round London, pushing him into deserted building sites and luring him into taxis. Von Einem seems to command a battalion of German officers, and Schwabing keeps scores of gillies and a monoplane in Galloway on the off-chance that somebody would need to be hunted over the moors. These villains are able to operate as monarchs of crime, seeking to destroy a civilisation that has lost, in Lumley's words, 'its one great power – the terror of God and his Church'. They are a cerebral corporation, 'nameless brains, working silently in the background', occasionally producing 'some cataclysmic revelation' – such as the Great War itself. 'Some day there will come the marriage of knowledge and will, and then the world will march', Lumley says. The dark forces are internationalised, or, as we might say nowadays, globalised. To the fore are international unions of workers and meetings of middle-class intellectuals. Worst of all is their 'half-scientific, half-philosophic jargon . . . dear . . . to the hearts of the half-baked'. Very true, of course, and the thinness of the crust of civilisation, whatever that may nowadays be, is as relevant in our time as it was when Buchan was writing in the early war-torn years of the twentieth century. This book's intoxicating blend of madness with scents of home and countryside must have appealed powerfully to fighting men facing the one and longing for the other. It is easy to see why.

Stella Rimington
May 2007

My Dear General,

A recent tale of mine has, I am told, found favour in the dug-outs and billets of the British front, as being sufficiently short and sufficiently exciting for men who have little leisure to read. My friends in that uneasy region have asked for more. So I have printed this story, written in the smooth days before the war, in the hope that it may enable an honest man here and there to forget for an hour the too urgent realities. I have put your name on it, because among the many tastes which we share, one is a liking for precipitous yarns.

J.B.

PREFACE BY THE EDITOR

We were at Glenaicill – six of us – for the duck-shooting, when Leithen told us this story. Since five in the morning we had been out on the skerries, and had been blown home by a wind which threatened to root the house and its wind-blown woods from their precarious lodgment on the hill. A vast nondescript meal, luncheon and dinner in one, had occupied us till the last daylight departed, and we settled ourselves in the smoking-room for a sleepy evening of talk and tobacco.

Conversation, I remember, turned on some of Jim's trophies which grinned at us from the firelit walls, and we began to spin hunting yarns. Then Hoppy Bynge, who was killed next year on the Bramaputra, told us some queer things about his doings in New Guinea, where he tried to climb Carstensz, and lived for six months in mud. Jim said he couldn't abide mud – anything was better than a country where your boots rotted. (He was to get enough of it last winter in the Ypres Salient.) You know how one tale begets another, and soon the whole place hummed with odd recollections, for five of us had been a good deal about the world.

All except Leithen, the man who was afterwards Solicitor-General, and, they say, will get to the Woolsack in time. I don't suppose he had ever been farther from home than Monte Carlo, but he liked hearing about the ends of the earth.

Jim had just finished a fairly steep yarn about his experiences on a Boundary Commission near Lake Chad, and Leithen got up to find a drink.

'Lucky devils,' he said. 'You've had all the fun out of life. I've had my nose to the grindstone ever since I left school.'

I said something about his having all the honour and glory.

'All the same,' he went on, 'I once played the chief part in a rather exciting business without ever once budging from London. And the joke of it was that the man who went out to look for adventure only saw a bit of the game, and I who sat in my chambers saw it all and pulled the strings. "They also serve who only stand and wait," you know.'

Then he told us this story. The version I give is one he afterwards wrote down, when he had looked up his diary for some of the details.

ONE

Beginning of the Wild-Goose Chase

It all started one afternoon early in May when I came out of the House of Commons with Tommy Deloraine. I had got in by an accident at a by-election, when I was supposed to be fighting a forlorn hope, and as I was just beginning to be busy at the Bar I found my hands pretty full. It was before Tommy succeeded, in the days when he sat for the family seat in Yorkshire, and that afternoon he was in a powerful bad temper. Out of doors it was jolly spring weather; there was greenery in Parliament Square and bits of gay colour, and a light wind was blowing up from the river. Inside a dull debate was winding on, and an advertising member had been trying to get up a row with the Speaker. The contrast between the frowsy place and the cheerful world outside would have impressed even the soul of a Government Whip.

Tommy sniffed the spring breeze like a supercilious stag.

'This about finishes me,' he groaned. 'What a juggins I am to be mouldering here! Joggleberry is the celestial limit, what they call in happier lands the pink penultimate. And the frowst on those back benches! Was there ever such a moth-eaten old museum?'

'It is the Mother of Parliaments,' I observed.

'Damned monkey-house,' said Tommy. 'I must get off for a bit or I'll bonnet Joggleberry or get up and propose a national monument to Guy Fawkes or something silly.'

I did not see him for a day or two, and then one morning he rang me up and peremptorily summoned me to dine with him. I went, knowing very well what I should find. Tommy was off next day to shoot lions on the Equator, or something equally unconscientious. He was a bad acquaintance for a placid, sedentary soul like me, for though he could work like a Trojan when the fit took him, he was never at the same job very long. In the same week he would harass an Under-Secretary about horses for the Army, write voluminously to the press about a gun he had invented for potting aeroplanes, give a fancy-dress ball which he forgot to attend, and get into the semi-final of the racquets championship. I waited daily to see him start a new religion.

That night, I recollect, he had an odd assortment of guests. A Cabinet Minister was there, a gentle being for whom Tommy professed public scorn and private affection; a sailor; an Indian cavalry fellow; Chapman, the Labour member, whom Tommy called Chipmunk; myself, and old Milson of the Treasury. Our host was in tremendous form, chaffing everybody, and sending Chipmunk into great rolling gusts of merriment. The two lived adjacent in Yorkshire, and on platforms abused each other like pickpockets.

Tommy enlarged on the misfits of civilised life. He maintained that none of us, except perhaps the sailor and the cavalryman, were at our proper jobs. He would have had Wytham – that was the Minister – a cardinal of the Roman Church, and he said that Milson should have been the Warden of a college full of port and prejudice. Me he was kind enough to allocate to some reconstructed Imperial General Staff, merely because I had a craze for military history. Tommy's perception did not go very deep. He told

Chapman he should have been a lumberman in California. 'You'd have made an uncommon good logger, Chipmunk, and you know you're a dashed bad politician.'

When questioned about himself he became reticent, as the newspapers say. 'I doubt if I'm much good at any job,' he confessed, 'except to ginger up my friends. Anyhow I'm getting out of this hole. Paired for the rest of the session with a chap who has lockjaw. I'm off to stretch my legs and get back my sense of proportion.'

Someone asked him where he was going, and was told 'Venezuela, to buy Government bonds and look for birds' nests.'

Nobody took Tommy seriously, so his guests did not trouble to bid him the kind of farewell a prolonged journey would demand. But when the others had gone, and we were sitting in the little back smoking-room on the first floor, he became solemn. Portentously solemn, for he wrinkled up his brows and dropped his jaw in the way he had when he fancied he was in earnest.

'I've taken on a queer job, Leithen,' he said, 'and I want you to hear about it. None of my family know, and I would like to leave some one behind me who could get on to my tracks if things got troublesome.'

I braced myself for some preposterous confidence, for I was experienced in Tommy's vagaries. But I own to being surprised when he asked me if I remembered Pitt-Heron.

I remembered Pitt-Heron very well. He had been at Oxford with me, but he was no great friend of mine, though for about two years Tommy and he had been inseparable. He had had a prodigious reputation for cleverness with every-body but the college authorities, and used to spend his vacations doing mad things in the Alps and the Balkans, and writing about them in the halfpenny press. He was enormously rich – cottonmills and Liverpool ground-rents – and being without a father, did pretty much what his fantastic taste dictated. He was rather a hero for a bit after he came down, for he had made some wild journey in the neighbourhood of Afghanistan, and written an exciting book about it.

Then he married a pretty cousin of Tommy's, who happened to be the only person that ever captured my stony heart, and settled down in London. I did not go to their house, and soon I found that very few of his friends saw much of him either. His travels and magazine articles suddenly stopped, and I put it down to the common course of successful domesticity. Apparently I was wrong.

'Charles Pitt-Heron,' said Tommy, 'is blowing up for a most thundering mess.'

I asked what kind of mess, and Tommy said he didn't know. 'That's the mischief of it. You remember the wild beggar he used to be, always off on the spree to the Mountains of the Moon or somewhere. Well, he has been damping down his fires lately, and trying to behave like a respectable citizen, but God knows what he has been thinking! I go a good deal to Portman Square, and all last year he has been getting queerer.'

Questions as to the nature of the queerness only elicited the fact that Pitt-Heron had taken to science with some enthusiasm.

'He has got a laboratory at the back of the house – used to be the billiard-room – where he works away half the night. And Lord! The crew you meet there! Every kind of heathen – Chinese and Turks, and long-haired chaps from Russia, and fat Germans. I've several times blundered into the push. They've all got an odd secretive air about them, and Charlie is becoming like them. He won't answer a plain question or look you straight in the face. Ethel sees it too, and she has often talked to me about it.'

I said I saw no harm in such a hobby.

'I do,' said Tommy grimly. 'Anyhow, the fellow has bolted.'

'What on earth—' I began, but was cut short.

'Bolted without a word to a mortal soul. He told Ethel he would be home for luncheon yesterday, and never came. His man knew nothing about him, hadn't packed for him or anything; but he found he had stuffed some things into a kitbag and gone out by the back through the mews. Ethel was in terrible straits and sent for me, and I ranged all yesterday afternoon like a wolf on the scent. I found he had drawn a biggish sum in gold from the bank, but I couldn't find any trace of where he had gone.

'I was just setting out for Scotland Yard this morning when Tomlin, the valet, rang me up and said he had found a card in the waistcoat of the dress clothes that Charles had worn the night before he left. It had a name on it like Konalevsky, and it struck me that they might know something about the business at the Russian Embassy. Well, I went round there, and the long and short of it was that I found there was a fellow of that name among the clerks. I saw him, and he said he had gone to see Mr Pitt-Heron two days before with a letter from some Embassy chap. Unfortunately the man in question had gone off to New York next day, but Konalevsky told me one thing which helped to clear up matters. It seemed that the letter had been one of those passports that Embassies give to their friends – a higher-powered sort than the ordinary make – and Konalevsky gathered from something he had heard that Charles was aiming at Moscow.'

Tommy paused to let his news sink in.

'Well, that was good enough for me. I'm off tomorrow to run him to ground.'

'But why shouldn't a man go to Moscow if he wants?' I said feebly.

'You don't understand,' said the sage Tommy. 'You don't know old Charles as I know him. He's got into a queer set, and there's no knowing what mischief he's up to. He's perfectly capable of starting a revolution in Armenia or somewhere merely to see how it feels like to be a revolutionary. That's the damned thing about the artistic temperament. Anyhow, he's got to chuck it. I won't have Ethel scared to death by his whims. I am going to hale him back from Moscow, even if I have to pretend he's an escaped lunatic. He's probably like enough one by this time if he has taken no clothes.'

I have forgotten what I said, but it was some plea for caution. I could not see the reason for these heroics. Pitt-Heron did not interest me greatly, and the notion of Tommy as a defender of the hearth amused me. I thought that he was working on very slight evidence, and would probably make a fool of himself.

'It's only another of the man's fads,' I said. 'He never could do things like an ordinary mortal. What possible trouble could there be? Money?'

'Rich as Croesus,' said Tommy.

'A woman?'

'Blind as a bat to female beauty.'

'The wrong side of the law?'

'Don't think so. He could settle any ordinary scrape with a cheque.'

'Then I give it up. Whatever it is, it looks as if Pitt-Heron would have a companion in misfortune before you are done with the business. I'm all for you taking a holiday, for at present you are a nuisance to your friends and a disgrace to your country's legislature. But for goodness' sake curb your passion for romance. They don't like it in Russia.'

Next morning Tommy turned up to see me in Chambers. The prospect of travel always went to his head like wine. He was in wild spirits, and had forgotten his anger at the defaulting Pitt-Heron in gratitude for his provision of an occupation. He talked of carrying him off to the Caucasus when he had found him, to investigate the habits of the Caucasian stag.

I remember the scene as if it were yesterday. It was a hot May morning, and the sun which came through the dirty window in Fountain Court lit up the dust and squalor of my working chambers. I was pretty busy at the time, and my table was well nourished with briefs. Tommy picked up one and began to read it. It was about a new drainage scheme in West Ham. He tossed it down and looked at me pityingly.

'Poor old beggar!' he said. 'To spend your days on such work when the world is chock-full of amusing things. Life goes roaring by and you only hear the echo in your stuffy rooms. You can hardly see the sun for the cobwebs on these windows of yours. Charles is a fool, but I'm blessed if he isn't wiser than you. Don't you wish you were coming with me?'

The queer thing was that I did. I remember the occasion, as I have said, for it was one of the few on which I have had a pang of dissatisfaction with the calling I had chosen. As Tommy's footsteps grew faint on the stairs I suddenly felt as if I were missing something, as if somehow I were out of it. It is an unpleasant feeling even when you know that the thing you are out of is foolishness.

Tommy went off at eleven from Victoria, and my work was

pretty well ruined for the day. I felt oddly restless, and the cause was not merely Tommy's departure. My thoughts kept turning to the Pitt-Herons – chiefly to Ethel, that adorable child unequally yoked to a perverse egoist, but a good deal to the egoist himself. I have never suffered much from whimsies, but I suddenly began to feel a curious interest in the business – an unwilling interest, for I found it in my heart to regret my robust scepticism of the night before. And it was more than interest. I had a sort of presentiment that I was going to be mixed up in the affair more than I wanted. I told myself angrily that the life of an industrious common-law barrister could have little to do with the wanderings of two maniacs in Muscovy. But, try as I might, I could not get rid of the obsession. That night it followed me into my dreams, and I saw myself with a knout coercing Tommy and Pitt-Heron in a Russian fortress which faded away into the Carlton Hotel.

Next afternoon I found my steps wending in the direction of Portman Square. I lived at the time in Down Street, and I told myself I would be none the worse of a walk in the Park before dinner. I had a fancy to see Mrs Pitt-Heron, for, though I had only met her twice since her marriage, there had been a day when we were the closest of friends.

I found her alone, a perplexed and saddened lady with imploring eyes. Those eyes questioned me as to how much I knew. I told her presently that I had seen Tommy and was aware of his errand. I was moved to add that she might count on me if there were anything she wished done on this side of the Channel.

She was very little changed. There was still the old exquisite slimness, the old shy courtesy. But she told me nothing. Charles was full of business and becoming very forgetful. She was sure the Russian journey was all a stupid mistake. He probably thought he had told her of his departure. He would write; she expected a letter by every post.

But her haggard eyes belied her optimism. I could see that there had been odd happenings of late in the Pitt-Heron household. She either knew or feared something – the latter, I thought, for her air was more of apprehension than of painful enlightenment.

I did not stay long, and, as I walked home, I had an awkward feeling that I had intruded. Also I was increasingly certain that there was trouble brewing, and that Tommy had more warrant for his journey than I had given him credit for. I cast my mind back to gather recollections of Pitt-Heron, but all I could find was an impression of a brilliant, uncomfortable being, who had been too fond of the byways of life for my sober tastes. There was nothing crooked in him in the wrong sense, but there might be a good deal that was perverse. I remember consoling myself with the thought that, though he might shatter his wife's nerves by his vagaries, he would scarcely break her heart.

To be watchful, I decided, was my business. And I could not get rid of the feeling that I might soon have cause for all my vigilance.

TWO

I First Hear of Mr Andrew Lumley

A fortnight later – to be accurate, on the 21st of May – I did a thing I rarely do, and went down to South London on a County Court case. It was an ordinary taxi-cab accident, and, as the solicitors for the company were good clients of mine and the regular County Court junior was ill in bed, I took the case to oblige them. There was the usual dull conflict of evidence. An empty taxi-cab, proceeding slowly on the right side of the road and hooting decorously at the corners, had been run into by a private motor-car which had darted down a side street. The taxi had been swung round and its bonnet considerably damaged, while its driver had suffered a dislocated shoulder. The bad feature in the case was that the motor-car had not halted to investigate the damage, but had proceeded unconscientiously on its way, and the assistance of the London police had been called in to trace it. It turned out to be the property of a Mr Julius Pavia, a retired East India merchant, who lived in a large villa in the neighbourhood of Blackheath, and at the time of the accident it had been occupied by his butler. The company brought an action for damages against its owner.

The butler, Tuke by name, was the only witness for the defence. He was a tall man, with a very long, thin face, and a jaw, the two parts of which seemed scarcely to fit. He was profuse in his apologies on behalf of his master, who was abroad. It seemed that on the morning in question – it was the 8th of May – he had received instructions from Mr Pavia to convey a message to a passenger by the Continental express from Victoria, and had been hot on this errand when he met the taxi. He was not aware that there had been any damage, thought it only a slight grazing of the two cars, and on his master's behalf consented to the judgment of the court.

It was a commonplace business, but Tuke was by no means a commonplace witness. He was very unlike the conventional butler, much liker one of those successful financiers whose portraits you see in the picture papers. His little eyes were quick with intelligence, and there were lines of ruthlessness around his mouth, like those of a man often called to decisive action. His story was simplicity itself, and he answered my questions with an air of serious candour. The train he had to meet was the 11a.m. from Victoria, the train by which Tommy had travelled. The passenger he had to see was an American gentleman, Mr Wright Davies. His master, Mr Pavia, was in Italy, but would shortly be home again.

The case was over in twenty minutes, but it was something unique in my professional experience. For I took a most intense and unreasoning dislike to that bland butler. I cross-examined with some rudeness, was answered with steady courtesy, and hopelessly snubbed. The upshot was that I lost my temper, to the surprise of the County Court judge. All the way back I was both angry and ashamed of myself. Half-way home I realised that the accident had happened on the very day that Tommy left London. The coincidence merely flickered across my mind, for there could be no earthly connection between the two events.

That afternoon I wasted some time in looking up Pavia in the directory. He was there sure enough as the occupier of a suburban mansion called the White Lodge. He had no city address, so it was clear that he was out of business. My irritation with the man had made me inquisitive about the master. It was a curious name he bore, possibly Italian, possibly Goanese. I wondered how he got on with his highly competent butler. If Tuke had been my servant I would have wrung his neck or bolted before a week was out.

Have you ever noticed that, when you hear a name that strikes you, you seem to be constantly hearing it for a bit? Once I had a case in which one of the parties was called Jubber, a name I had never met before, but I ran across two other Jubbers before the case was over. Anyhow, the day after the Blackheath visit I was briefed in a big Stock Exchange case, which turned on the true ownership of certain bearer bonds. It was a complicated business, which I need not trouble you with, and it involved a number of consultations with my lay clients, a famous firm of brokers. They produced their books, and my chambers were filled with glossy gentlemen talking a strange jargon.

I had to examine my clients closely on their practice in treating a certain class of bearer security, and they were very frank in expounding their business. I was not surprised to hear that Pitt-Heron was one of the most valued names on their lists. With his wealth he was bound to be a good deal in the city. Now I had no desire to pry into Pitt-Heron's private affairs, especially his financial arrangements, but his name was in my thoughts at the time, and I could not help looking curiously at what was put before me. He seemed to have been buying these bonds on a big scale. I had the indiscretion to ask if Mr Pitt-Heron had long followed this course, and was told that he had begun to purchase some six months before.

'Mr Pitt-Heron,' volunteered the stockbroker, 'is very closely connected in his financial operations with another esteemed client of ours, Mr Julius Pavia. They are both attracted by this class of security.'

At the moment I scarcely noted the name, but after dinner that night I began to speculate about the connection. I had found out the name of one of Charles's mysterious new friends. It was not a very promising discovery. A retired East India merchant did not suggest anything wildly speculative, but I began to wonder if Charles's preoccupation, to which Tommy had been witness, might not be connected with financial worries. I could not believe that the huge Pitt-Heron fortunes had been seriously affected, or that his flight was that of a defaulter, but he might have got entangled in some shady city business which preyed on his sensitive soul. Somehow or other I could not believe that Mr Pavia was a wholly innocent old gentleman; his butler looked too formidable. It was possible that he was blackmailing Pitt-Heron, and that the latter had departed to get out of his clutches.

But on what ground? I had no notion as to the blackmailable thing that might lurk in Charles's past, and the guesses which flitted through my brain were too fantastic to consider seriously. After all, I had only the flimsiest basis for conjecture. Pavia and Pitt-Heron were friends; Tommy had gone off in quest of Pitt-Heron; Pavia's butler had broken the law of the land in order, for some reason or other, to see the departure of the train by which Tommy had travelled. I remember laughing at myself for my suspicions, and reflecting that, if Tommy could see into my head, he would turn a deaf ear in the future to my complaints of his lack of balance.

But the thing stuck in my mind, and I called again that week on Mrs Pitt-Heron. She had had no word from her husband, and only a bare line from Tommy, giving his Moscow address. Poor child, it was a wretched business for her. She had to keep a smiling face to the world, invent credible tales to account for her husband's absence, and all the while anxiety and dread were gnawing at her heart. I asked her if she had ever met a Mr Pavia, but the name was unknown to her. She knew nothing of Charles's business dealings, but at my request she interviewed his bankers, and I heard from her next day that his affairs were in perfect order. It was no financial crisis which had precipitated him abroad.

A few days later I stumbled by the merest accident upon what sailors call a 'cross-bearing'. At the time I used to 'devil' a little for the Solicitor-General, and 'note' cases sent to him from the different Government offices. It was thankless work, but it was supposed to be good for an ambitious lawyer. By this prosaic channel I received the first hint of another of Charles's friends.

I had sent me one day the papers dealing with the arrest of a German spy at Plymouth, for at the time there was a sort of epidemic of roving Teutons, who got themselves into compromising situations, and gravely troubled the souls of the Admiralty and the War Office. This case was distinguished from the common ruck by the higher social standing of the accused. Generally the spy is a photographer or bag-man who attempts to win the bibulous confidence of minor officials. But this specimen was no less than a professor of a famous German university, a man of excellent manners, wide culture, and attractive presence, who had dined with Port officers and danced with Admirals' daughters. I have forgotten the evidence, or what was the legal point submitted for

the Law Officers' opinion; in any case it matters little, for he
was acquitted. What interested me at the time were the
testimonials as to character which he carried with him.
He had many letters of introduction. One was from Pitt-
Heron to his wife's sailor uncle; and when he was arrested
one Englishman went so far as to wire that he took upon
himself the whole costs of the defence. This gentleman was a
Mr Andrew Lumley, stated in the papers sent me to be a rich
bachelor, a member of the Athenaeum and Carlton Clubs,
and a dweller in the Albany.

Remember that, till a few weeks before, I had known
nothing of Pitt-Heron's circle, and here were three bits of
information dropping in on me unsolicited, just when my
interest had been awakened. I began to get really keen, for
every man at the bottom of his heart believes that he is a born
detective. I was on the look-out for Charles's infrequent
friends, and I argued that if he knew the spy and the spy
knew Mr Lumley, the odds were that Pitt-Heron and Lumley
were acquaintances. I hunted up the latter in the Red Book.
Sure enough he lived in the Albany, belonged to half a dozen
clubs, and had a country house in Hampshire.

I tucked the name away in a pigeon-hole of my memory,
and for some days asked every one I met if he knew the
philanthropist of the Albany. I had no luck till the Saturday,
when, lunching at the club, I ran against Jenkinson, the art
critic.

I forget if you know that I have always been a bit of a
connoisseur in a mild way. I used to dabble in prints and
miniatures, but at that time my interest lay chiefly in Old
Wedgwood, of which I had collected some good pieces. Old
Wedgwood is a thing which few people collect seriously, but
the few who do are apt to be monomaniacs. Whenever a big

collection comes into the market it fetches high prices, but it generally finds its way into not more than half a dozen hands. Wedgwoodites all know each other, and they are less cut-throat in their methods than most collectors. Of all I have ever met Jenkinson was the keenest, and he would discourse for hours on the 'feel' of good jasper, and the respective merits of blue and sage-green grounds.

That day he was full of excitement. He babbled through luncheon about the Wentworth sale, which he had attended the week before. There had been a pair of magnificent plaques, with a unique Flaxman design, which had roused his enthusiasm. Urns and medallions and whatnot had gone to this or that connoisseur, and Jenkinson could quote their prices, but the plaques dominated his fancy, and he was furious that the nation had not acquired them. It seemed that he had been to South Kensington and the British Museum, and all sorts of dignitaries, and he thought he might yet persuade the authorities to offer for them if the purchaser would resell. They had been bought by Lutrin for a well-known private collector, by name Andrew Lumley.

I pricked up my ears and asked about Mr Lumley.

Jenkinson said he was a rich old buffer who locked up his things in cupboards and never let the public get a look at them. He suspected that a lot of the best things at recent sales had found their way to him, and that meant that they were put in cold storage for good.

I asked if he knew him.

No, he told me, but he had once or twice been allowed to look at his things for books he had been writing. He had never seen the man, for he always bought through agents, but he had heard of people who knew him. 'It is the old silly game,' he said. 'He will fill half a dozen houses with priceless treasures, and then die, and the whole show will be sold at auction and the best things carried off to America. It's enough to make a patriot swear.'

There was balm in Gilead, however. Mr Lumley apparently might be willing to resell the Wedgwood plaques if he got a fair offer. So Jenkinson had been informed by Lutrin, and that very afternoon he was going to look at them. He asked me to come with him, and, having nothing to do, I accepted.

Jenkinson's car was waiting for us at the club door. It was closed, for the afternoon was wet. I did not hear his directions to the chauffeur, and we had been on the road ten minutes or so before I discovered that we had crossed the river and were traversing South London. I had expected to find the things in Lutrin's shop, but to my delight I was told that Lumley had taken delivery of them at once.

'He keeps very few of his things in the Albany except his books,' I was told. 'But he has a house at Blackheath which is stuffed from cellar to garret.'

'What is the name of it?' I asked with a sudden suspicion.

'The White Lodge,' said Jenkinson.

'But that belongs to a man called Pavia,' I said.

'I can't help that. The things in it belong to old Lumley, all right. I know, for I've been three times there with his permission.'

Jenkinson got little out of me for the rest of the ride. Here was excellent corroborative evidence of what I had allowed myself to suspect. Pavia was a friend of Pitt-Heron; Lumley was a friend of Pitt-Heron; Lumley was obviously a friend of Pavia, and he might be Pavia himself, for the retired East India merchant, as I figured him, would not be above an innocent impersonation. Anyhow, if I could find one or the other, I might learn something about Charles's recent doings. I sincerely hoped that the owner might be at home that afternoon when we inspected his treasures, for so far I had found no one who could procure me an introduction to that mysterious old bachelor of artistic and philo-Teutonic tastes.

We reached the White Lodge about half-past three. It was one of those small, square, late-Georgian mansions which you see all around London – once a country-house among fields, now only a villa in a pretentious garden. I looked to see my super-butler Tuke, but the door was opened by a female servant who inspected Jenkinson's card of admission, and somewhat unwillingly allowed us to enter.

My companion had not exaggerated when he described the place as full of treasures. It was far more like the shop of a Bond Street art-dealer than a civilised dwelling. The hall was crowded with Japanese armour and lacquer cabinets. One room was lined from floor to ceiling with good pictures, mostly seventeenth-century Dutch, and had enough Chippendale chairs to accommodate a public meeting. Jenkinson would fain have prowled round, but we were moved on by the inexorable servant to the little back room where lay the objects of our visit. The plaques had been only half-unpacked, and in a moment Jenkinson was busy on them with a magnifying glass, purring to himself like a contented cat.

The housekeeper stood on guard by the door, Jenkinson was absorbed, and after the first inspection of the treasures I had leisure to look about me. It was an untidy little room, full of fine Chinese porcelain in dusty glass cabinets, and in a corner stood piles of old Persian rugs.

Pavia, I reflected, must be an easy-going soul, entirely oblivious of comfort, if he allowed his friend to turn his dwelling into such a pantechnicon. Less and less did I believe in the existence of the retired East India merchant. The house was Lumley's, who chose to pass under another name during his occasional visits. His motive might be innocent enough, but somehow I did not think so. His butler had looked too infernally intelligent.

With my foot I turned over the lid of one of the packing-cases that had held the Wedgwoods. It was covered with a litter of cotton-wool and shavings, and below it lay a crumpled piece of paper. I looked again, and saw that it was a telegraph form. Clearly somebody, with the telegram in his hand, had opened the cases, and had left it on the top of one, whence it had dropped to the floor, and been covered by the lid when it was flung off.

I hope and believe that I am as scrupulous as other people, but then and there came on me the conviction that I must read that telegram. I felt the gimlet eye of the housekeeper on me, so I had recourse to craft. I took out my cigarette case as if to smoke, and clumsily upset its contents amongst the shavings. Then on my knees I began to pick them up, turning over the litter till the telegram was exposed.

It was in French, and I read it quite clearly. It had been sent from Vienna, but the address was in some code. '*Suivez à Bokhare Saronov*' – these were the words. I finished my collection of the cigarettes, and turned the lid over again on the telegram, so that its owner, if he chose to look for it diligently, might find it.

When we sat in the car going home, Jenkinson absorbed in meditation on the plaques, I was coming to something like a decision. A curious feeling of inevitability possessed me. I had collected by accident a few odd, disjointed pieces of information, and here by the most amazing accident of all was the connecting link. I knew I had no evidence to go upon which would have convinced the most credulous common jury. Pavia knew Pitt-Heron; so probably did Lumley. Lumley knew Pavia, possibly was identical with him. Somebody in Pavia's house got a telegram in which a trip to Bokhara was indicated. It didn't sound much. Yet I was absolutely convinced, with the queer subconscious certitude of the human brain, that Pitt-Heron was or was about to be in Bokhara, and that Pavia-Lumley knew of his being there and was deeply concerned in his journey.

That night after dinner I rang up Mrs Pitt-Heron.

She had had a letter from Tommy, a very dispirited letter, for he had had no luck. Nobody in Moscow had seen or heard of any wandering Englishman remotely like Charles; and Tommy, after playing the private detective for three weeks, was nearly at the end of his tether and spoke of returning home.

I told her to send him the following wire in her own name: '*Go on to Bokhara. Have information you will meet him there.*'

She promised to send the message next day, and asked no further questions. She was a pearl among women.

THREE

Tells of a Midsummer Night

Hitherto I had been the looker-on; now I was to become a person of the drama. That telegram was the beginning of my active part in this curious affair. They say that everybody turns up in time at the corner of Piccadilly Circus if you wait long enough. I was to find myself like a citizen of Baghdad in the days of the great Caliph, and yet never stir from my routine of flat, chambers, club, flat.

I am wrong: there was one episode out of London, and that perhaps was the true beginning of my story.

Whitsuntide that year came very late, and I was glad of the fortnight's rest, for Parliament and the Law Courts had given me a busy time. I had recently acquired a car and a chauffeur called Stagg, and I looked forward to trying it in a tour in the West Country. But before I left London I went again to Portman Square.

I found Ethel Pitt-Heron in grave distress. You must remember that Tommy and I had always gone on the hypothesis that Charles's departure had been in pursuance of some mad scheme of his own which might get him into trouble. We thought that he had become mixed up with highly undesirable friends, and was probably embarking in some venture which might not be criminal but was certain to be foolish. I had long rejected the idea of blackmail, and convinced myself that Lumley and Pavia were his colleagues.

The same general notion, I fancy, had been in his wife's mind. But now she had found something which altered the case.

She had ransacked his papers in the hope of finding a clue to the affair which had taken him abroad, but there was nothing but business letters, notes of investments, and such-like. He seemed to have burned most of his papers in the queer laboratory at the back of the house. But, stuffed into the pocket of a blotter on a bureau in the drawing-room where he scarcely ever wrote, she had found a document. It seemed to be the rough draft of a letter, and it was addressed to her. I give it as it was written; the blank spaces were left blank in the manuscript.

> You must have thought me mad, or worse, to treat you as I have done. But there was a terrible reason, which some day I hope to tell you all about. I want you as soon as you get this to make ready to come out to me at . . . You will travel by . . . and arrive at . . . I enclose a letter which I want you to hand in deepest confidence to Knowles, the solicitor. He will make all arrangements about your journey and about sending me the supplies of money I want. Darling, you must leave as secretly as I did, and tell nobody anything, not even that I am alive – that least of all. I would not frighten you for worlds, but I am on the edge of a horrible danger, which I hope with God's help and yours to escape . . .

That was all – obviously the draft of a letter which he intended to post to her from some foreign place. But can you conceive a missive more calculated to shatter a woman's nerves? It filled me, I am bound to say, with heavy disquiet.

Pitt-Heron was no coward, and he was not the man to make too much of a risk. Yet it was clear that he had fled that day in May under the pressure of some mortal fear.

The affair in my eyes began to look very bad. Ethel wanted me to go to Scotland Yard, but I dissuaded her. I have the utmost esteem for Scotland Yard, but I shrank from publicity at this stage. There might be something in the case too delicate for the police to handle, and I thought it better to wait.

I reflected a great deal about the Pitt-Heron business the first day or two of my trip, but the air and the swift motion helped me to forget it. We had a fortnight of superb weather, and sailed all day through a glistening green country under the hazy blue heavens of June. Soon I fell into the blissful state of physical and mental ease which such a life induces. Hard toil, such as deer-stalking, keeps the nerves on the alert and the mind active, but swimming all day in a smooth car through a heavenly landscape mesmerises brain and body.

We ran up the Thames valley, explored the Cotswolds, and turned south through Somerset till we reached the fringes of Exmoor. I stayed a day or two at a little inn high up in the moor, and spent the time tramping the endless ridges of hill or scrambling in the arbutus thickets where the moor falls in steeps to the sea. We returned by Dartmoor and the south coast, meeting with our first rain in Dorset, and sweeping into sunlight again on Salisbury Plain. The time came when only two days remained to me. The car had behaved beyond all my hopes, and Stagg, a sombre and silent man, was lyrical in its praise.

I wanted to be in London by the Monday afternoon, and to insure this I made a long day of it on the Sunday. It was the

long day which brought our pride to a fall. The car had run so
well that I resolved to push on and sleep in a friend's house
near Farnham. It was about half-past eight, and we were
traversing the somewhat confused and narrow roads in the
neighbourhood of Wolmer Forest, when, as we turned a
sharp corner, we ran full into the tail of a heavy carrier's cart.
Stagg clapped on the brakes, but the collision, though it did
no harm to the cart, was sufficient to send the butt-end of
something through our glass screen, damage the tyre of the
near front wheel, and derange the steering-gear. Neither of
us suffered much hurt, but Stagg got a long scratch on his
cheek from broken glass, and I had a bruised shoulder.

The carrier was friendly but useless, and there was nothing
for it but to arrange for horses to take the car to Farnham.
This meant a job of some hours, and I found on inquiry at a
neighbouring cottage that there was no inn where I could
stay within eight miles. Stagg borrowed a bicycle somehow
and went off to collect horses, while I morosely reviewed the
alternatives before me.

I did not like the prospect of spending the June night
beside my derelict car, and the thought of my friend's house
near Farnham beckoned me seductively. I might have walked
there, but I did not know the road, and I found that my
shoulder was paining me, so I resolved to try to find some
gentleman's house in the neighbourhood where I could
borrow a conveyance. The south of England is now so densely
peopled by Londoners that even in a wild district, where there
are no inns and few farms, there are certain to be several
week-end cottages.

I walked along the white ribbon of road in the scented June
dusk. At first it was bounded by high gorse, then came
patches of open heath, and then woods. Beyond the woods I

found a park railing, and presently an entrance-gate with a lodge. It seemed to be the place I was looking for, and I woke the lodge-keeper, who thus early had retired to bed. I asked the name of the owner, but was told the name of the place instead – it was High Ashes. I asked if the owner was at home, and got a sleepy nod for answer.

The house, as seen in the half-light, was a long white-washed cottage, rising to two storeys in the centre. It was plentifully covered with creepers and roses, and the odour of flowers was mingled with the faintest savour of wood-smoke, pleasant to a hungry traveller in the late hours. I pulled an old-fashioned bell, and the door was opened by a stolid young parlour-maid.

I explained my errand, and offered my card. I was, I said, a Member of Parliament and of the Bar, who had suffered a motor accident. Would it be possible for the master of the house to assist me to get to my destination near Farnham? I was bidden to enter, and wearily seated myself on a settle in the hall.

In a few minutes an ancient housekeeper appeared, a grim dame whom at other times I should have shunned. She bore, however, a hospitable message. There was no conveyance in the place, as the car had gone that day to London for repairs. But if I cared to avail myself of the accommodation of the house for the night it was at my service. Meantime my servant could be looking after the car, and a message would go to him to pick me up in the morning.

I gratefully accepted, for my shoulder was growing troublesome, and was conducted up a shallow oak staircase to a very pleasant bedroom with a bathroom adjoining. I had a bath, and afterwards found a variety of comforts put at my service from slippers to razors. There was also some Elliman for my wounded shoulder. Clean and refreshed I made my way downstairs and entered a room from which I caught a glow of light.

It was a library, the most attractive I think I have ever seen. The room was long, as libraries should be, and entirely lined with books, save over the fireplace, where hung a fine picture which I took to be a Raeburn. The books were in glass cases, which showed the beautiful shallow mouldings of a more artistic age. A table was laid for dinner in a corner, for the room was immense, and the shaded candlesticks on it, along with the late June dusk, gave such light as there was. At first I thought the place was empty, but as I crossed the floor a figure rose from a deep chair by the hearth.

'Good evening, Mr Leithen,' a voice said. 'It is a kindly mischance which gives a lonely old man the pleasure of your company.'

He switched on an electric lamp, and I saw before me what I had not guessed from the voice, an old man. I was thirty-four at the time, and counted anything over fifty old, but I judged my host to be well on in the sixties. He was about my own size, but a good deal bent in the shoulders, as if from study. His face was clean-shaven and extraordinarily fine, with every feature delicately chiselled. He had a sort of Hapsburg mouth and chin, very long and pointed, but modelled with a grace which made the full lower lip seem entirely right. His hair was silver, brushed so low on the forehead as to give him a slightly foreign air, and he wore tinted glasses, as if for reading.

Altogether it was a very dignified and agreeable figure who greeted me in a voice so full and soft that it belied his obvious age.

Dinner was a light meal, but perfect in its way. There were soles, I remember, an exceedingly well-cooked chicken, fresh strawberries, and a savoury. We drank a '95 Perrier-Jouet and some excellent Madeira. The stolid parlour-maid waited on us, and, as we talked of the weather and the Hampshire roads, I kept trying to guess my host's profession. He was not a lawyer, for he had not the inevitable lines on the cheek. I thought that he might be a retired Oxford don, or one of the higher civil servants, or perhaps some official of the British Museum. His library proclaimed him a scholar, and his voice a gentleman.

Afterwards we settled ourselves in armchairs, and he gave me a good cigar. We talked about many things – books, the right furnishing of a library, a little politics, in deference to my M.P.-ship. My host was apathetic about party questions, but curious about defence matters, and in his way an amateur strategist. I could fancy his indicting letters to *The Times* on national service.

Then we wandered into foreign affairs, where I found his interest acute, and his knowledge immense. Indeed he was so well informed that I began to suspect that my guesses had been wrong, and that he was a retired diplomat. At that time there was some difficulty between France and Italy over customs duties, and he sketched for me with remarkable clearness the weak points in the French tariff administration.

I had been recently engaged in a big South American railway case, and I asked him a question about the property of my clients. He gave me a much better account than I had ever got from the solicitors who briefed me.

The fire had been lit before we finished dinner, and presently it began to burn up and light the figure of my host, who sat in a deep armchair. He had taken off his tinted glasses, and as I rose to get a match I saw his eyes looking abstractedly before him.

Somehow they reminded me of Pitt-Heron. Charles had always a sort of dancing light in his, a restless intelligence which was at once attractive and disquieting. My host had this and more. His eyes were paler than I had ever seen in a human head – pale, bright, and curiously wild. But, whereas Pitt-Heron's had only given the impression of reckless youth, this man's spoke of wisdom and power as well as of endless vitality.

All my theories vanished, for I could not believe that my host had ever followed any profession. If he had, he would have been at the head of it, and the world would have been familiar with his features. I began to wonder if my recollection was not playing me false, and I was in the presence of some great man whom I ought to recognise.

As I dived into the recesses of my memory I heard his voice asking if I were not a lawyer.

I told him, Yes. A barrister with a fair common-law practice and some work in Privy Council appeals.

He asked me why I chose the profession.

'It came handiest,' I said. 'I am a dry creature, who loves facts and logic. I am not a flier, I have no new ideas, I don't want to lead men, and I like work. I am the ordinary educated Englishman, and my sort gravitates to the Bar. We like feeling that, if we are not the builders, at any rate we are the cement of civilisation.'

He repeated the words 'cement of civilisation' in his soft voice.

'In a sense you are right. But civilisation needs more than the law to hold it together. You see, all mankind are not equally willing to accept as divine justice what is called human law.'

'Of course there are further sanctions,' I said. 'Police and armies and the goodwill of civilisation.'

He caught me up quickly. 'The last is your true cement. Did you ever reflect, Mr Leithen, how precarious is the tenure of the civilisation we boast about?'

'I should have thought it fairly substantial,' I said, 'and – the foundations grow daily firmer.'

He laughed. 'That is the lawyer's view, but, believe me, you are wrong. Reflect, and you will find that the foundations are sand. You think that a wall as solid as the earth separates civilisation from barbarism. I tell you the division is a thread, a sheet of glass. A touch here, a push there, and you bring back the reign of Saturn.' It was the kind of paradoxical, undergraduate speculation which grown men indulge in sometimes after dinner. I looked at my host to discover his mood, and at the moment a log flared up again.

His face was perfectly serious. His light wild eyes were intently watching me.

'Take one little instance,' he said. 'We are a commercial world, and have built up a great system of credit. Without our cheques and bills of exchange and currency the whole of our life would stop. But credit only exists because behind it we have a standard of value. My Bank of England notes are worthless paper unless I can get sovereigns for them if I choose. Forgive this elementary disquisition, but the point is important. We have fixed a gold standard, because gold is sufficiently rare, and because it allows itself to be coined into a portable form. I am aware that there are economists who say that the world could be run equally well on a pure credit basis, with no metal currency at the back of it; but, however sound their argument may be in the abstract, the thing is practically impossible. You would have to convert the whole of the world's stupidity to their economic faith before it would work.

'Now, suppose something happened to make our standard of value useless. Suppose the dream of the alchemists came true, and all metals were readily transmutable. We have got very near it in recent years, as you will know if you interest yourself in chemical science. Once gold and silver lost their intrinsic value, the whole edifice of our commerce would collapse. Credit would become meaningless, because it would be untranslatable. We should be back at a bound in the age of barter, for it is hard to see what other standard of value could take the place of the precious metals. All our civilisation, with its industries and commerce, would come toppling down. Once more, like primitive man, I would plant cabbages for a living, and exchange them for services in kind from the cobbler and the butcher. We should have the simple life with a vengeance, not the self-conscious simplicity of the civilised man, but the compulsory simplicity of the savage.'

I was not greatly impressed by the illustration. 'Of course there are many key-points in civilisation,' I said, 'and the loss of them would bring ruin. But those keys are strongly held.'

'Not so strongly as you think. Consider how delicate the machine is growing. As life grows more complex, the machinery grows more intricate, and therefore more vulnerable. Your so-called sanctions become so infinitely numerous that each in itself is frail. In the Dark Ages you had one great power – the terror of God and His Church. Now you have a multiplicity of small things, all delicate and fragile, and strong only by our tacit agreement not to question them.'

'You forget one thing,' I said, 'the fact that men really are agreed to keep the machine going. That is what I called the "goodwill of civilisation".'

He got up from his chair and walked up and down the floor, a curious dusky figure lit by the rare spurts of flame from the hearth.

'You have put your finger on the one thing that matters. Civilisation is a conspiracy. What value would your police be if every criminal could find a sanctuary across the Channel, or your law courts, if no other tribunal recognised their decisions? Modern life is the silent compact of comfortable folk to keep up pretences. And it will succeed till the day comes when there is another compact to strip them bare.'

I do not think that I have ever listened to a stranger conversation. It was not so much what he said – you will hear the same thing from any group of half-baked young men – as the air with which he said it. The room was almost dark, but the man's personality seemed to take shape and bulk in the gloom. Though I could scarcely see him, I knew that those pale, strange eyes were looking at me. I wanted more light, but did not know where to look for a switch. It was all so eerie and odd that I began to wonder if my host were not a little mad. In any case, I was tired of his speculations.

'We won't dispute on the indisputable,' I said. 'But I should have thought that it was the interest of all the best brains of the world to keep up what you call the conspiracy.'

He dropped into his chair again.

'I wonder,' he said slowly. 'Do we really get the best brains working on the side of the compact? Take the business of Government. When all is said, we are ruled by the amateurs and the second-rate. The methods of our departments would bring any private firm to bankruptcy. The methods of Parliament – pardon me – would disgrace any board of directors. Our rulers pretend to buy expert knowledge, but they never pay the price for it that a businessman would pay, and if they get it they have not the courage to use it. Where is the inducement for a man of genius to sell his brains to our insipid governors?

'And yet knowledge is the only power – now as ever. A little mechanical device will wreck your navies. A new chemical combination will upset every rule of war. It is the same with our commerce. One or two minute changes might sink Britain to the level of Ecuador, or give China the key of the world's wealth. And yet we never dream that these things are possible. We think our castles of sand are the ramparts of the universe.'

I have never had the gift of the gab, but I admire it in others. There is a morbid charm in such talk, a kind of exhilaration, of which one is half ashamed. I found myself interested, and more than a little impressed.

'But surely,' I said, 'the first thing a discoverer does is to make his discovery public. He wants the honour and glory, and he wants money for it. It becomes part of the world's knowledge, and everything is readjusted to meet it. That was what happened with electricity. You call our civilisation a machine, but it is something far more flexible. It has the power of adaptation of a living organism.'

'That might be true if the new knowledge really became the world's property. But does it? I read now and then in the papers that some eminent scientist has made a great discovery. He reads a paper before some Academy of Science, and there are leading articles in it, and his photograph adorns the magazines. That kind of man is not the danger. He is a bit of the machine, a party to the compact. It is the men who stand outside it that are to be reckoned with, the artists in discovery who will never use their knowledge till they can use it with full effect. Believe me, the biggest brains are without the ring which we call civilisation.'

Then his voice seemed to hesitate. 'You may hear people say that submarines have done away with the battleship, and that aircraft have annulled the mastery of the sea. That is what our pessimists say. But do you imagine that the clumsy submarine or the fragile aeroplane is really the last word of science?'

'No doubt they will develop,' I said, 'but by that time the power of the defence will have advanced also.'

He shook his head. 'It is not so. Even now the knowledge which makes possible great engines of destruction is far beyond the capacity of any defence. You see only the productions of second-rate folk who are in a hurry to get wealth and fame. The true knowledge, the deadly knowledge, is still kept secret. But, believe me, my friend, it is there.'

He paused for a second, and I saw the faint outline of the smoke from his cigar against the background of the dark. Then he quoted me one or two cases, slowly, as if in some doubt about the wisdom of his words.

It was these cases that startled me. They were of different kinds – a great calamity, a sudden breach between two nations, a blight on a vital crop, a war, a pestilence. I will not repeat them. I do not think I believed in them then, and now I believe less. But they were horribly impressive, as told in that quiet voice in that sombre room on that dark June night. If he was right, these things had not been the work of Nature or accident, but of a devilish art. The nameless brains that he spoke of, working silently in the background, now and then showed their power by some cataclysmic revelation. I did not believe him, but, as he put the case, showing with strange clearness the steps in the game, I had no words to protest.

At last I found my voice.

'What you describe is super-anarchy, and yet it makes no headway. What is the motive of those diabolical brains?'

He laughed. 'How should I be able to tell you? I am a humble inquirer, and in my researches I come on curious bits of fact. But I cannot pry into motives. I only know of the existence of great extra-social intelligences. Let us say that they distrust the machine. They may be idealists and desire to make a new world, or they may simply be artists, loving for its own sake the pursuit of truth. If I were to hazard a guess, I should say that it took both types to bring about results, for the second find the knowledge and the first the will to use it.'

A recollection came back to me. It was of a hot upland meadow in Tyrol, where among acres of flowers and beside a leaping stream I was breakfasting after a morning spent in climbing the white crags. I had picked up a German on the way, a small man of the Professor class, who did me the honour to share my sandwiches. He conversed fluently but quaintly in English, and he was, I remember, a Nietzschean and a hot rebel against the established order. 'The pity,' he cried, 'is that the reformers do not know, and those who know are too idle to reform. Some day there will come the marriage of knowledge and will, and then the world will march.'

'You draw an awful picture,' I said. 'But if those extra-social brains are so potent, why after all do they effect so little? A dull police-officer, with the machine behind him, can afford to laugh at most experiments in anarchy.'

'True,' he said, 'and civilisation will win until its enemies learn from it the importance of the machine. The compact must endure until there is a counter-compact. Consider the ways of that form of foolishness which today we call nihilism or anarchy. A few illiterate bandits in a Paris slum defy the world, and in a week they are in jail. Half a dozen crazy Russian intellectuals in Geneva conspire to upset the Romanovs, and are hunted down by the police of Europe. All the Governments and their not very intelligent police forces join hands, and hey, presto! there is an end of the conspirators. For civilisation knows how to use such powers as it has, while the immense potentiality of the unlicensed is dissipated in vapour. Civilisation wins because it is a worldwide league; its enemies fail because they are parochial. But supposing . . .'

Again he stopped and rose from his chair. He found a switch and flooded the room with light. I glanced up blinking to see my host smiling down on me, a most benevolent and courteous old gentleman. He had resumed his tinted glasses. 'Forgive me,' he said, 'for leaving you in darkness while I bored you with my gloomy prognostications. A recluse is apt to forget what is due to a guest.'

He handed the cigar-box to me, and pointed to a table where whisky and mineral waters had been set out.

'I want to hear the end of your prophecies,' I said. 'You were saying—?'

'I said – supposing anarchy learned from civilisation and became international. Oh, I don't mean the bands of advertising donkeys who call themselves International Unions of Workers and such-like rubbish. I mean if the real brainstuff of the world were internationalised. Suppose that the links in the cordon of civilisation were neutralised by other links in a far more potent chain. The earth is seething with incoherent power and unorganised intelligence. Have you ever reflected on the case of China? There you have millions of quick brains stifled in trumpery crafts. They have no direction, no driving power, so the sum of their efforts is futile, and the world laughs at China. Europe throws her a million or two on loan now and then, and she cynically responds by begging the prayers of Christendom. And yet, I say, supposing—'

'It's a horrible idea,' I said, 'and, thank God, I don't believe it possible. Mere destruction is too barren a creed to inspire a new Napoleon, and you can do with nothing short of one.'

'It would scarcely be destruction,' he replied gently. 'Let us call it iconoclasm, the swallowing of formulas, which has always had its full retinue of idealists. And you do not want a Napoleon. All that is needed is direction, which could be given by men of far lower gifts than a Bonaparte. In a word, you want a Power-House, and then the age of miracles will begin.'

I got up, for the hour was late, and I had had enough of this viewy talk. My host was smiling, and I think that smile was the thing I really disliked about him. It was too – what shall I say, – superior and Olympian.

As he led me into the hall he apologised for indulging his whims. 'But you, as a lawyer, should welcome the idea. If there is an atom of truth in my fancies, your task is far bigger than you thought. You are not defending an easy case, but fighting in a contest where the issues are still doubtful. That should encourage your professional pride.'

By all the rules I should have been sleepy, for it was past midnight, and I had had a long day in the open air. But that wretched talk had unsettled me, and I could not get my mind off it. I have reproduced very crudely the substance of my host's conversation, but no words of mine could do justice to his eerie persuasiveness. There was a kind of magnetism in the man, a sense of vast powers and banked-up fires, which would have given weight to the tritest platitudes. I had a horrible feeling that he was trying to convince me, to fascinate me, to prepare the ground for some proposal. Again and again I told myself it was crazy nonsense, the heated dream of a visionary, but again and again I came back to some detail which had a horrid air of reality. If the man was a romancer he had an uncommon gift of realism.

I flung open my bedroom window and let in the soft air of the June night and the scents from leagues of clover and pines and sweet grasses. It momentarily refreshed me, for I could not believe that this homely and gracious world held such dire portents.

But always that phrase of his, the 'Power-House,' kept recurring. You know how twisted your thoughts get during a wakeful night, and long before I fell asleep towards morning I had worked myself up into a very complete dislike of that bland and smiling gentleman, my host. Suddenly it occurred to me that I did not know his name, and that set me off on another train of reflection.

I did not wait to be called, but rose about seven, dressed, and went downstairs. I heard the sound of a car on the gravel of the drive, and to my delight saw that Stagg had arrived. I wanted to get away from the house as soon as possible, and I had no desire to meet its master again in this world.

The grim housekeeper, who answered my summons, received my explanation in silence. Breakfast would be ready in twenty minutes; eight was Mr Lumley's hour for it.

'Mr Andrew Lumley?' I asked with a start.

'Mr Andrew Lumley,' she said.

So that was my host's name. I sat down at a bureau in the hall and did a wildly foolish thing.

I wrote a letter, beginning 'Dear Mr Lumley', thanking him for his kindness and explaining the reason of my early departure. It was imperative, I said, that I should be in

London by midday. Then I added: 'I wish I had known who you were last night, for I think you know an old friend of mine, Charles Pitt-Heron.'

Breakfastless I joined Stagg in the car, and soon we were swinging down from the uplands to the shallow vale of the Wey. My thoughts were very little on my new toy or on the midsummer beauties of Surrey. The friend of Pitt-Heron, who knew about his going to Bokhara, was the maniac who dreamed of the 'Power-House'. There were going to be dark scenes in the drama before it was played out.

FOUR

I Follow the Trail of the Super-Butler

My first thought, as I journeyed towards London, was that I was horribly alone in this business.

Whatever was to be done I must do it myself, for the truth was I had no evidence which any authority would recognise. Pitt-Heron was the friend of a strange being who collected objects of art, probably passed under an alias in South London, and had absurd visions of the end of civilisation. That, in cold black and white, was all my story came to. If I went to the police they would laugh at me, and they would be right.

Now I am a sober and practical person, but, slender though my evidence was, it brought to my mind the most absolute conviction. I seemed to know Pitt-Heron's story as if I had heard it from his own lips – his first meeting with Lumley and their growing friendship; his initiation into secret and forbidden things; the revolt of the decent man, appalled that his freakishness had led him so far; the realisation that he could not break so easily with his past, and that Lumley held him in his power; and last, the mad flight under the pressure of overwhelming terror.

I could read, too, the purpose of that flight. He knew the Indian frontier as few men know it, and in the wild tangle of the Pamirs he hoped to baffle his enemy. Then from some far refuge he would send for his wife, and spend the rest of his days in exile. It must have been an omnipotent terror to drive such a man, young, brilliant, rich, successful, to the fate of an absconding felon.

But Lumley was on his trail. So I read the telegram I had picked up on the floor of the Blackheath house, and my business was to frustrate the pursuit. Some one must have gone to Bokhara, some creature of Lumley's, perhaps the super-butler I had met in the County Court. The telegram, for I had noted the date, had been received on the 27th day of May. It was now the 15th of June, so if some one had started immediately on its receipt, in all probability he would by now be in Bokhara.

I must find out who had gone, and endeavour to warn Tommy. I calculated that it would have taken him seven or eight days to get from Moscow by the Transcaspian; probably he would find Pitt-Heron gone, but inquiries would set him on the track. I might be able to get in touch with him through the Russian officials. In any case, if Lumley were stalking Pitt-Heron, I, unknown and unsuspected, would be stalking Lumley.

And then in a flash I realised my folly.

The wretched letter I had written that morning had given the whole show away. Lumley knew that I was a friend of Pitt-Heron, and that I knew that he was a friend of Pitt-Heron. If my guess was right, friendship with Lumley was not a thing Charles was likely to confess to, and he would argue that my knowledge of it meant that I was in Charles's confidence. I would therefore know of his disappearance and its cause, and alone in London would connect it with the decorous bachelor of the Albany. My letter was a warning to him that he could not play the game unobserved, and I, too, would be suspect in his eyes.

It was no good crying over spilt milk, and Lumley's suspicions must be accepted. But I confess that the thought gave me the shivers. The man had a curious terror for me, a terror I cannot hope to analyse and reproduce for you. My bald words can give no idea of the magnetic force of his talk, the sense of brooking an unholy craft. I was proposing to match my wits against a master's – one, too, who must have at his command an organisation far beyond my puny efforts. I have said that my first feeling was that of loneliness and isolation; my second was one of hopeless insignificance. It was a boy's mechanical toy arrayed against a Power-House with its shining wheels and monstrous dynamos.

My first business was to get into touch with Tommy.

At that time I had a friend in one of the Embassies, whose acquaintance I had made on a dry-fly stream in Hampshire. I will not tell you his name, for he has since become a great figure in the world's diplomacy, and I am by no means certain that the part he played in this tale was strictly in accordance with official etiquette. I had assisted him on the legal side in some of the international worries that beset all Embassies, and we had reached the point of intimacy which is marked by the use of Christian names and by dining frequently together. Let us call him Monsieur Felix. He was a grave young man, slightly my senior, learned, discreet, and ambitious, but with an engaging boyishness cropping up now and then under the official gold lace. It occurred to me that in him I might find an ally.

I reached London about eleven in the morning, and went straight to Belgrave Square. Felix I found in the little library off the big secretaries' room, a sunburnt sportsman fresh from a Norwegian salmon-river. I asked him if he had half an hour to spare, and was told that the day was at my service.

'You know Tommy Deloraine?' I asked.

He nodded.

'And Charles Pitt-Heron?'

'I have heard of him.'

'Well, here is my trouble. I have reason to believe that Tommy has joined Pitt-Heron in Bokhara. If he has, my mind will be greatly relieved, for, though I can't tell you the story, I can tell you that Pitt-Heron is in very considerable danger. Can you help me?'

Felix reflected. 'That should be simple enough. I can wire in cypher to the Military Governor. The police there are pretty efficient, as you may imagine, and travellers don't come and go without being remarked. I should be able to give you an answer within twenty-four hours. But I must describe Tommy. How does one do that in telegraphese?'

'I want you to tell me another thing,' I said. 'You remember that Pitt-Heron has some reputation as a Central Asian traveller. Tommy, as you know, is as mad as a hatter. Suppose these two fellows at Bokhara, wanting to make a long trek into wild country – how would they go? You've been there, and know the lie of the land.'

Felix got down a big German atlas, and for half an hour we pored over it. From Bokhara, he said, the only routes for madmen ran to the south. East and north you got into Siberia; west lay the Transcaspian desert; but southward you might go through the Hissar range by Pamirski Post to Gilgit and Kashmir, or you might follow up the Oxus and enter the north of Afghanistan, or you might go by Merv into north-eastern Persia. The first he thought the likeliest route, if a man wanted to travel fast.

I asked him to put in his cable a suggestion about watching

the Indian roads, and left him with a promise of early enlightenment.

Then I went down to the Temple, fixed some consultations, and spent a quiet evening in my rooms. I had a heavy sense of impending disaster, not unnatural in the circumstances. I really cannot think what it was that held me to the job, for I don't mind admitting that I felt pretty queasy about it. Partly, no doubt, liking for Tommy and Ethel, partly regret for that unfortunate fellow Pitt-Heron, most of all, I think, dislike of Lumley. That bland superman had fairly stirred my prosaic antipathies.

That night I went carefully over every item in the evidence to try and decide on my next step. I had got to find out more about my enemies. Lumley, I was pretty certain, would baffle me, but I thought I might have a better chance with the super-butler. As it turned out, I hit his trail almost at once.

Next day I was in a case at the Old Bailey. It was an important prosecution for fraud, and I appeared, with two leaders, for the bank concerned. The amazing and almost incredible thing about this story of mine is the way clues kept rolling in unsolicited, and I was to get another from this dull prosecution. I suppose that the explanation is that the world is full of clues to everything, and that if a man's mind is sharp-set on any quest, he happens to notice and take advantage of what otherwise he would miss. My leaders were both absent the first day, and I had to examine our witnesses alone.

Towards the close of the afternoon I put a fellow in the box, an oldish, drink-sodden clerk from a Cannon Street bucket-shop. His evidence was valuable for our case, but I was very doubtful how he would stand a cross-examination as to credit. His name was Routh, and he spoke with a strong north-country accent. But what caught my attention was his face. His jaw looked as if it had been made in two pieces which did not fit, and he had little, bright, protuberant eyes. At my first glance I was conscious of a recollection.

He was still in the box when the Court rose, and I informed the solicitors that before going further I wanted a conference with the witness. I mentioned also that I should like to see him alone. A few minutes later he was brought to my chambers, and I put one or two obvious questions on the case, till the managing clerk who accompanied him announced with many excuses that he must hurry away. Then I shut the door, gave Mr Routh a cigar, and proceeded to conduct a private inquiry.

He was a pathetic being, only too ready to talk. I learned the squalid details of his continuous misfortunes. He had been the son of a dissenting minister in Northumberland, and had drifted through half a dozen occupations till he found his present unsavoury billet. Truth was written large on his statement; he had nothing to conceal, for his foible was folly, not crime, and he had not a rag of pride to give him reticence. He boasted that he was a gentleman and well-educated, too, but he had never had a chance. His brother had advised him badly; his brother was too clever for a prosaic world; always through his reminiscences came this echo of fraternal admiration and complaint.

It was about the brother I wanted to know, and Mr Routh was very willing to speak. Indeed, it was hard to disentangle facts from his copious outpourings. The brother had been an engineer and a highly successful one; had dallied with politics, too, and had been a great inventor. He had put Mr Routh on to a South American speculation, where he had made a little money, but speedily lost it again. Oh, he had been a good brother in his way, and had often helped him, but he was a busy man, and his help never went quite far enough. Besides, he did not like to apply to him too often. I gathered that the brother was not a person to take liberties with.

I asked him what he was doing now.

'Ah,' said Mr Routh, 'that is what I wish I could tell you. I will not conceal from you that for the moment I am in considerable financial straits, and this case, though my hands are clean enough, God knows, will not make life easier for me. My brother is a mysterious man, whose business often takes him abroad. I have never known even his address, for I write always to a London office from which my communications are forwarded. I only know that he is in some big electrical business, for I remember that he once let drop the remark that he was in charge of some power station. No, I do not think it is in London; probably somewhere abroad. I heard from him a fortnight ago, and he told me he was just leaving England for a couple of months. It is very annoying, for I want badly to get into touch with him.'

'Do you know, Mr Routh,' I said, 'I believe I have met your brother. Is he like you in any way?'

'We have a strong family resemblance, but he is taller and slimmer. He has been more prosperous, and has lived a healthier life, you see.'

'Do you happen to know,' I asked, 'if he ever uses another name? I don't think that the man I knew was called Routh.'

The clerk flushed. 'I think it highly unlikely that my brother would use an alias. He has done nothing to disgrace a name of which we are proud.'

I told him that my memory had played me false, and we parted on very good terms. He was an innocent soul, one of those people that clever rascals get to do their dirty work for them. But there was no mistaking the resemblance. There, without the brains and force and virility, went my super-butler of Blackheath, who passed under the name of Tuke.

The clerk had given me the name of the office to whose address he had written to his brother. I was not surprised to find that it was that of the firm of stockbrokers for whom I was still acting in the bearer-bonds case where I had heard Pavia's name.

I rang up the partner whom I knew, and told him a very plausible story of having a message for one of Mr Pavia's servants, and asked him if he were in touch with them and could forward letters. He made me hold the line, and then came back and told me that he had forwarded letters for Tuke, the butler, and one Routh who was a groom or foot-man. Tuke had gone abroad to join his master and he did not know his address. But he advised me to write to the White Lodge.

I thanked him and rang off. That was settled, anyhow. Tuke's real name was Routh, and it was Tuke who had gone to Bokhara.

My next step was to ring up Macgillivray at Scotland Yard and get an appointment in half an hour's time. Macgillivray had been at the Bar – I had read in his chambers – and was now one of the heads of the Criminal Investigation Depart-ment. I was about to ask him for information which he was in no way bound to give me, but I presumed on our old acquaintance. I asked him first whether he had ever heard of a secret organisation which went under the name of the Power-House. He laughed out loud at my question.

'I should think we have several hundreds of such pet names on our records,' he said. 'Everything from the Lodge of the Baldfaced Ravens to Solomon's Seal No. X. Fancy nomenclature is the relaxation of the tired anarchist, and matters very little. The dangerous fellows have no names, no numbers even, which we can get hold of. But I'll get a man to look up our records. There may be something filed about your Power-House.'

My second question he answered differently. 'Routh! Routh! Why, yes, there was a Routh we had dealings with a dozen years ago when I used to go the North-Eastern circuit. He was a trade-union official who bagged the funds, and they couldn't bring him to justice because of the ridiculous extra-legal status they possess. He knew it, and played their own privileges against them. Oh yes, he was a very complete rogue. I once saw him at a meeting in Sunderland, and I remember his face – sneering eyes, diabolically clever mouth, and with it all as smug as a family butler. He has disappeared from England – at least we haven't heard of him for some years, but I can show you his photograph.'

Macgillivray took from a lettered cabinet a bundle of cards, selected one, and tossed it towards me. It was that of a man of thirty or so, with short side-whiskers and a drooping moustache. The eyes, the ill-fitting jaw, and the brow were those of my friend Mr Tuke, brother and patron of the sorrowful Mr Routh, who had already that afternoon occupied my attention.

Macgillivray promised to make certain inquiries, and I walked home in a state of elation. Now I knew for certain who had gone to Bokhara, and I knew something, too, of the traveller's past. A discredited genius was the very man for Lumley's schemes – one who asked for nothing better than to use his brains outside the ring-fence of convention. Somewhere in the wastes of Turkestan the ex-trade-union official was in search of Pitt-Heron. I did not fancy that Mr Tuke would be very squeamish.

I dined at the club and left early. Going home, I had an impression that I was being shadowed.

You know the feeling that someone is watching you, a sort of sensation which the mind receives without actual evidence. If the watcher is behind, where you can't see him, you have a cold feeling between your shoulders. I daresay it is a legacy from the days when the cave-man had to look pretty sharp to keep from getting his enemy's knife between the ribs.

It was a bright summer evening, and Piccadilly had its usual crowd of motor-cars and buses and foot passengers. I halted twice, once in St James's Street and once at the corner of Stratton Street, and retraced my steps for a bit; and each time I had the impression that someone a hundred yards or so off had done the same. My instinct was to turn round and face him, whoever he was, but I saw that that was foolishness. Obviously in such a crowd I could get no certainty in the matter, so I put it out of my mind.

I spent the rest of the evening in my rooms, reading cases and trying to keep my thoughts off Central Asia. About ten I was rung up on the telephone by Felix. He had had his answer from Bokhara. Pitt-Heron had left with a small caravan on June 2nd by the main road through the Hissar range. Tommy had arrived on June 10th, and on the 12th had set off with two servants on the same trail. Travelling the lighter of the two, he should have overtaken Pitt-Heron by the 15th at latest.

That was yesterday, and my mind was immensely relieved. Tommy in such a situation was a tower of strength, for, whatever his failings in politics, I knew no one I would rather have with me to go tiger-shooting.

Next day the sense of espionage increased. I was in the habit of walking down to the Temple by way of Pall Mall and the Embankment, but, as I did not happen to be in Court that morning, I resolved to make a detour and test my suspicions. There seemed to be nobody in Down Street as I emerged from my flat, but I had not walked five yards before, turning back, I saw a man enter from the Piccadilly end, while another moved across the Hertford Street opening. It may have been only my imagination, but I was convinced that these were my watchers.

I walked up Park Lane, for it seemed to me that by taking the Tube at the Marble Arch Station I could bring matters to the proof. I have a knack of observing small irrelevant details, and I happened to have noticed that a certain carriage in the train which left Marble Arch about nine thirty stopped exactly opposite the exit at the Chancery Lane Station, and by hurrying up the passage one could just catch the lift which served an earlier train, and so reach the street before any of the other travellers.

I performed this manoeuvre with success, caught the early lift, reached the street, and took cover behind a pillar-box, from which I could watch the exit of passengers from the stairs. I judged that my tracker, if he missed me below, would run up the stairs rather than wait on the lift. Sure enough, a breathless gentleman appeared, who scanned the street eagerly, and then turned to the lift to watch the emerging passengers. It was clear that the espionage was no figment of my brain.

I walked slowly to my chambers, and got through the day's work as best I could, for my mind was preoccupied with the unpleasant business in which I found myself entangled. I would have given a year's income to be honestly quit of it, but

there seemed to be no way of escape. The maddening thing
was that I could do so little. There was no chance of forgetting
anxiety in strenuous work. I could only wait with the patience
at my command, and hope for the one chance in a thousand
which I might seize. I felt miserably that it was no game for
me. I had never been brought up to harry wild beasts and risk
my neck twice a day at polo like Tommy Deloraine. I was a
peaceful sedentary man, a lover of a quiet life, with no
appetite for perils and commotions. But I was beginning
to realise that I was very obstinate.

At four o'clock I left the Temple and walked to the
Embassy. I had resolved to banish the espionage from my
mind, for that was the least of my difficulties.

Felix gave me an hour of his valuable time. It was something that Tommy had joined Pitt-Heron, but there were
other matters to be arranged in that far country. The time had
come, in my opinion, to tell him the whole story.

The telling was a huge relief to my mind. He did not laugh
at me as I had half feared, but took the whole thing as gravely
as possible. In his profession, I fancy, he had found too many
certainties behind suspicions to treat anything as trivial. The
next step, he said, was to warn the Russian police of the
presence of the man called Saronov and the super-butler.
Happily we had materials for the description of Tuke or
Routh, and I could not believe that such a figure would be
hard to trace. Felix cabled again in cypher, asking that the two
should be watched, more especially if there was reason to
believe that they had followed Tommy's route. Once more we
got out the big map and discussed the possible ways. It
seemed to me a land created by Providence for surprises, for
the roads followed the valleys, and to the man who travelled
light there must be many short cuts through the hills.

I left the Embassy before six o'clock and, crossing the Square engrossed with my own thoughts, ran full into Lumley.

I hope I played my part well, though I could not repress a start of surprise. He wore a grey morning-coat and a white top-hat, and looked the image of benevolent respectability.

'Ah, Mr Leithen,' he said, 'we meet again.'

I murmured something about my regrets at my early departure three days ago, and added the feeble joke that I wished he would hurry on his Twilight of Civilisation, for the burden of it was becoming too much for me.

He looked me in the eyes with all the friendliness in the world. 'So you have not forgotten our evening's talk? You owe me something, my friend, for giving you a new interest in your profession.'

'I owe you much,' I said, 'for your hospitality, your advice, and your warnings.'

He was wearing his tinted glasses, and peered quizzically into my face.

'I am going to make a call in Grosvenor Place,' he said, 'and shall beg in return the pleasure of your company. So you know my young friend, Pitt-Heron?'

With an ingenuous countenance I explained that he had been at Oxford with me and that we had common friends.

'A brilliant young man,' said Lumley. 'Like you, he has occasionally cheered an old man's solitude. And he has spoken of me to you?'

'Yes,' I said, lying stoutly. 'He used to tell me about your collections.' (If Lumley knew Charles well he would find me out, for the latter would not have crossed the road for all the treasures of the Louvre.)

'Ah, yes, I have picked up a few things. If ever you should

care to see them I should be honoured. You are a connoisseur? Of a sort? You interest me, for I should have thought
your taste lay in other directions than the dead things of art.
Pitt-Heron is no collector. He loves life better than art, as a
young man should. A great traveller, our friend – the
Laurence Oliphant or Richard Burton of our day.'

We stopped at a house in Grosvenor Place, and he relin-
quished my arm. 'Mr Leithen,' he said, 'a word from one who
wishes you no ill. You are a friend of Pitt-Heron, but where
he goes you cannot follow. Take my advice and keep out of
his affairs. You will do no good to him, and you may bring
yourself into serious danger. You are a man of sense, a
practical man, so I speak to you frankly. But, remember, I do
not warn twice.'

He took off his glasses, and his light, wild eyes looked me
straight in the face. All benevolence had gone, and something implacable and deadly burned in them. Before I could
say a word in reply he shuffled up the steps of the house and
was gone.

FIVE

I Take a Partner

That meeting with Lumley scared me badly, but it also clinched my resolution. The most pacific fellow on earth can be gingered into pugnacity. I had now more than my friendship for Tommy and my sympathy with Pitt-Heron to urge me on. A man had tried to bully me, and that roused all the worst stubbornness of my soul. I was determined to see the game through at any cost.

But I must have an ally if my nerves were to hold out, and my mind turned at once to Tommy's friend, Chapman. I thought with comfort of the bluff independence of the Labour member. So that night at the House I hunted him out in the smoking-room.

He had been having a row with the young bloods of my party that afternoon and received me ungraciously.

'I'm about sick of you fellows,' he growled. (I shall not attempt to reproduce Chapman's accent. He spoke rich Yorkshire, with a touch of the drawl of the western dales.) 'They went and spoiled the best speech, though I say it as shouldn't, which this old place has heard for a twelvemonth. I've been workin' for days at it in the Library. I was tellin' them how much more bread cost under Protection, and the Jew Hilderstein started a laugh because I said kilometres for kilogrammes. It was just a slip o' the tongue, for I had it right in my notes, and besides, these furrin words don't matter a curse. Then that young lord as sits for East Claygate gets up and goes out as I was gettin' into my peroration, and he drops his topper and knocks off old Higgins's spectacles, and all the idiots laughed. After that I gave it them hot and strong, and got called to order. And then Wattles, him as used to be as good a Socialist as me, replied for the Government and his blamed Board, and said that the Board thought this and the Board thought that, and was blessed if the Board would stir its stumps. Well I mind the day when I was hanging on to the Board's coat-tails in Hyde Park to keep it from talking treason.'

It took me a long time to get Chapman settled down and anchored to a drink.

'I want you,' I said, 'to tell me about Routh – you know the fellow I mean – the ex-union-leader.'

At that he fairly blazed up.

'There you are, you Tories,' he shouted, causing a pale Liberal member on the next sofa to make a hurried exit. 'You can't fight fair. You hate the unions, and you rake up any rotten old prejudice to discredit them. You can find out about Routh for yourself, for I'm damned if I help you.'

I saw I could do nothing with Chapman unless I made a clean breast of it, so for the second time that day I told the whole story.

I couldn't have wished for a better audience. He got wildly excited before I was half through with it. No doubt of the correctness of my evidence ever entered his head, for, like most of his party, he hated anarchism worse than capitalism, and the notion of a highly-capitalised, highly-scientific, highly-undemocratic anarchism fairly revolted his soul. Besides, he adored Tommy Deloraine.

Routh, he told me, had been a young engineer of a

superior type, with a job in a big shop at Sheffield. He had professed advanced political views, and, although he had strictly no business to be there, had taken a large part in trade union work, and was treasurer of one big branch. Chapman had met him often at conferences and on platforms, and had been impressed by the fertility and ingenuity of his mind and the boldness of his purpose. He was the leader of the left wing of the movement, and had that gift of half-scientific, half-philosophic jargon which is dear at all times to the hearts of the half-baked. A seat in Parliament had been repeatedly offered him, but he had always declined; wisely, Chapman thought, for he judged him the type which is more effective behind the scenes.

But with all his ability he had not been popular. 'He was a cold-blooded, sneering devil,' as Chapman put it, 'a sort of Parnell. He tyrannised over his followers, and he was the rudest brute I ever met.'

Then followed the catastrophe, in which it became apparent that he had speculated with the funds of the union and had lost a large sum. Chapman, however, was suspicious of these losses, and was inclined to suspect that he had the money all the time in a safe place. A year or two earlier the unions, greatly to the disgust of old-fashioned folk, had been given certain extra-legal privileges, and this man Routh had been one of the chief advocates of the unions' claims. Now he had the cool effrontery to turn the tables on them, and use those very privileges to justify his action and escape prosecution.

There was nothing to be done. Some of the fellows, said Chapman, swore to wring his neck, but he did not give them the chance. He had disappeared from England, and was generally believed to be living in some foreign capital.

'What I would give to be even with the swine!' cried my friend, clenching and unclenching his big fist. 'But we're up against no small thing in Josiah Routh. There isn't a crime on earth he'd stick at, and he's as clever as the old Devil, his master.'

'If that's how you feel, I can trust you to back me up,' I said. 'And the first thing I want you to do is to come and stay at my flat. God knows what may happen next, and two men are better than one. I tell you frankly, I'm nervous, and I would like to have you with me.'

Chapman had no objection. I accompanied him to his Bloomsbury lodgings, where he packed a bag, and we returned to the Down Street flat. The sight of his burly figure and sagacious face was relief to me in the mysterious darkness where I now found myself walking.

Thus began my housekeeping with Chapman, one of the queerest episodes in my life. He was the best fellow in the world, but I found that I had misjudged his character. To see him in the House you would have thought him a piece of granite, with his Yorkshire bluntness and hard, downright, north-country sense. He had all that somewhere inside him, but he was also as romantic as a boy. The new situation delighted him. He was quite clear that it was another case of the strife between Capital and Labour – Tommy and I standing for Labour, though he used to refer to Tommy in public as a 'gilded popinjay,' and only a month before had described me in the House as a 'viperous lackey of Capitalism.' It was the best kind of strife in which you had not to meet your adversary with long-winded speeches, but might any moment get a chance to pummel him with your fists. He made me ache with laughter. The spying business used to rouse him to fury. I don't think he was tracked as I was, but he chose to fancy he was, and was guilty of assault and battery on one butcher's boy, two cabbies, and a gentleman who turned out to be a bookmaker's assistant. This side of him got to be an infernal nuisance, and I had many rows with him. Among other things, he chose to suspect my man Waters of treachery – Waters, who was the son of a gardener at home, and hadn't wits enough to put up an umbrella when it rained.

'You're not taking this business rightly,' he maintained one night. 'What's the good of waiting for these devils to down you? Let's go out and down them.' And he announced his intention, from which no words of mine could dissuade him, of keeping watch on Mr Andrew Lumley at the Albany.

His resolution led to a complete disregard of his Parliamentary duties. Deputations of constituents waited for him in vain. Of course he never got a sight of Lumley. All that happened was that he was very nearly given in charge more than once for molesting peaceable citizens in the neighbourhood of Piccadilly and Regent Street.

One night on my way home from the Temple I saw in the bills of the evening papers the announcement of the arrest of a Labour Member. It was Chapman, sure enough. At first I feared that he had got himself into serious trouble, and was much relieved to find him in the flat in a state of blazing anger. It seemed that he had found somebody whom he thought was Lumley, for he only knew him from my descriptions. The man was in a shop in Jermyn Street, with a car waiting outside, and Chapman had – politely, as he swore – asked the chauffeur his master's name. The chauffeur had replied abusively, upon which Chapman had hailed him from the driver's seat and shaken him till his teeth rattled. The owner came out, and Chapman was arrested and taken off to the nearest police-court. He had been compelled to apologise, and had been fined five pounds and costs.

By the mercy of Heaven the chauffeur's master was a money-lender of evil repute, so the affair did Chapman no harm. But I was forced to talk to him seriously. I knew it was no use explaining that for him to spy on the Power-House was like an elephant stalking a gazelle. The only way was to appeal to his incurable romanticism.

'Don't you see,' I told him, 'that you are playing Lumley's game? He will trap you sooner or later into some escapade which will land you in jail, and where will I be then? That is what he and his friends are out for. We have got to meet cunning with cunning, and lie low till we get our chance.'

He allowed himself to be convinced and handed over to me the pistol he had bought, which had been the terror of my life.

'All right,' he said, 'I'll keep quiet. But you promise to let me into the big scrap when it comes off.'

I promised. Chapman's notion of the grand finale was a Homeric combat in which he would get his fill of fisticuffs.

He was an anxiety, but all the same he was an enormous comfort. His imperturbable cheerfulness and his racy talk were the tonics I wanted. He had plenty of wisdom, too. My nerves were getting bad those days, and, whereas I had rarely touched the things before, I now found myself smoking cigarettes from morning till night. I am pretty abstemious, as you know, but I discovered to my horror that I was drinking far too many whisky-and-sodas. Chapman knocked me off all that, and got me back to a pipe and a modest nightcap. He did more, for he undertook to put me in training. His notion was that we should win in the end by superior muscles. He was a square, thick-set fellow, who had been a good middle-weight boxer. I could box a bit myself, but I improved mightily under his tuition. We got some gloves, and used to hammer each other for half an hour every morning. Then might have been seen the shameful spectacle of a rising barrister with a swollen lip and a black eye arguing in court and proceeding of an evening to his country's legislature, where he was confronted from the opposite benches by the sight of a Leader of the People in the same vulgar condition.

In those days I wanted all the relief I could get, for it was a beastly time. I knew I was in grave danger, so I made my will and went through the other doleful performances consequent on the expectation of a speedy decease. You see I had nothing to grip on, no clear job to tackle, only to wait on the off-chance, with an atmosphere of suspicion thickening around me. The spying went on – there was no mistake about that – but I soon ceased to mind it, though I did my best to give my watchers little satisfaction. There was a hint of bullying about the spying. It is disconcerting at night to have a man bump against you and look you greedily in the face.

I did not go again to Scotland Yard, but one night I ran across Macgillivray in the club.

He had something of profound interest to tell me. I had asked about the phrase, the 'Power-House'. Well, he had come across it, in the letter of a German friend, a private letter, in which the writer gave the results of his inquiries into a curious affair which a year before had excited Europe.

I have forgotten the details, but it had something to do with the Slav States of Austria and an Italian Students' Union, and it threatened at one time to be dangerous. Macgillivray's correspondent said that in some documents which were seized he found constant allusion to a thing called the *Krafthaus*, evidently the headquarters staff of the plot. And this same word *Krafthaus* had appeared elsewhere – in a sonnet of a poet-anarchist who shot himself in the slums of Antwerp, in the last ravings of more than one criminal, in the extraordinary testament of Professor M of Jena, who, at the age of thirty-seven, took his life after writing a strange mystical message to his fellow-citizens.

Macgillivray's correspondent concluded by saying that, in his opinion, if this *Krafthaus* could be found, the key would be discovered to the most dangerous secret organisation in the world. He added that he had some reason to believe that the motive power of the concern was English.

'Macgillivray,' I said, 'you have known me for some time, and I fancy you think me a sober and discreet person. Well, I believe I am on the edge of discovering the secret of your *Krafthaus*. I want you to promise me that if in the next week I send you an urgent message you will act on it, however fantastic it seems. I can't tell you more. I ask you to take me on trust, and believe that for anything I do I have tremendous reasons.'

He knit his shaggy grey eyebrows and looked curiously at me. 'Yes, I'll go bail for your sanity. It's a good deal to promise, but if you make an appeal to me, I will see that it is met.'

Next day I had news from Felix. Tuke and the man called Saronov had been identified. If you are making inquiries about anybody it is fairly easy to find those who are seeking for the same person, and the Russian police, in tracking Tommy and Pitt-Heron, had easily come on the two gentlemen who were following the same trail. The two had gone by Samarkand, evidently intending to strike into the hills by a shorter route than the main road from Bokhara. The frontier posts had been warned, and the stalkers had become the stalked.

That was one solid achievement, at any rate. I had saved Pitt-Heron from the worst danger, for first I had sent him Tommy, and now I had put the police on guard against his enemies. I had not the slightest doubt that enemies they were. Charles knew too much, and Tuke was the man appointed to reason with him, to bring him back, if possible, or if not – as Chapman had said – the ex-union leader was not the man to stick at trifles.

It was a broiling June, the London season was at its height, and I had never been so busy in the courts before. But that crowded and garish world was little more than a dream to me. I went through my daily tasks, dined out, went to the play, had consultations, talked to my fellows, but all the while I had the feeling that I was watching somebody else perform the same functions. I believe I did my work well, and I know I was twice complimented by the Court of Appeal.

But my real interests were far away. Always I saw two men in the hot glens of the Oxus, with the fine dust of the *loess* rising in yellow clouds behind them. One of these men had a drawn and anxious face, and both rode hard. They passed by the closes of apricot and cherry and the green watered gardens, and soon the Oxus ceased to flow wide among rushes and water-lilies and became a turbid hill-stream. By-and-by the roadside changed, and the horses of the travellers trod on mountain turf, crushing the irises and marigolds and thyme. I could feel the free air blowing from the roof of the world, and see far ahead the snowy saddle of the pass which led to India.

Far behind the riders I saw two others, and they chose a different way, now over waterless plateaux, now in rugged *nullahs*. They rode the faster and their route was the shorter. Sooner or later they must catch up the first riders, and I knew, though how I could not tell, that death would attend the meeting.

I, and only I, sitting in London four thousand miles away, could prevent disaster. The dream haunted me at night, and often, walking in the Strand or sitting at a dinner-table, I have found my eyes fixed clearly on the shining upland with the thin white mountains at the back of it, and the four dots, which were men, hurrying fast on their business.

One night I met Lumley. It was at a big political dinner given by the chief of my party in the House of Lords – fifty or sixty guests, and a blaze of stars and decorations. I sat near the bottom of the table, and he was near the top, sitting between a famous General and an ex-Viceroy of India. I asked my right-hand neighbour who he was, but he could not tell me. The same question to my left-hand neighbour brought an answer.

'It's old Lumley. Have you never met him? He doesn't go out much, but he gives a man's dinner now and then, which are the best in London. No. He's not a politician, though he favours our side, and I expect has given a lot to our funds. I can't think why they don't make him a Peer. He's enormously rich and very generous, and the most learned old fellow in Britain. My Chief' – my neighbour was an Under-Secretary – 'knows him, and told me once that if you wanted any out-of-the-way bit of knowledge you could get it by asking Lumley. I expect he pulls the strings more than anybody living. But he scarcely ever goes out, and it's a feather in our host's cap to have got him tonight. You never see his name in the papers, either. He probably pays the Press to keep him out, like some of those millionaire fellows in America.' I watched him through dinner. He was the centre of the talk at his end of the table. I could see the blue ribbon bulging out on Lord Morecambe's breast as he leaned forward to question him. He was wearing some foreign orders, including the Legion of Honour, and I could hear in the pauses of conversation echoes of his soft rich voice. I could see him beaming through his glasses on his neighbours, and now and then he would take them off and look mildly at a speaker. I wondered why nobody realised, as I did, what was in his light, wild eyes.

The dinner, I believe, was excellent, and the company was good, but down at my end I could eat little, and I did not want to talk. Here in this pleasant room, with servants moving softly about, and a mellow light on the silver from the shaded candles, I felt the man was buttressed and defended beyond my reach. A kind of despairing hatred gripped me when I looked his way. For I was always conscious of that other picture, the Asian desert, Pitt-Heron's hunted face, and the grim figure of Tuke on his trail. That, and the great secret wheels of what was too inhuman to be called crime, moving throughout the globe under this man's hand.

There was a party afterwards, but I did not stay. No more did Lumley, and for a second I brushed against him in the hall at the foot of the big staircase.

He smiled on me affectionately.

'Have you been dining here? I did not notice you.'

'You had better things to think of,' I said. 'By the way, you gave me good advice some weeks ago. It may interest you to hear that I have taken it.'

'I am so glad,' he said softly. 'You are a very discreet young man.'

But his eyes told me that he knew I lied.

SIX

The Restaurant in Antioch Street

I was working late at the Temple next day, and it was nearly seven before I got up to go home. Macgillivray had telephoned to me in the afternoon saying he wanted to see me and suggesting dinner at the club, and I had told him I should come straight there from my Chambers. But just after six he had rung me up again and proposed another meeting-place.

'I've got some very important news for you and want to be quiet. There's a little place where I sometimes dine – Rapaccini's, in Antioch Street. I'll meet you there at half-past seven.'

I agreed, and sent a message to Chapman at the flat, telling him I would be out to dinner. It was a Wednesday night, so the House rose early. He asked me where I was dining and I told him, but I did not mention with whom. His voice sounded very cross, for he hated a lonely meal. It was a hot, still night, and I had had a heavy day in Court, so heavy that my private anxieties had almost slipped from my mind. I walked along the Embankment, and up Regent Street towards Oxford Circus. Antioch Street, as I had learned from the directory, was in the area between Langham Place and Tottenham Court Road. I wondered vaguely why Macgillivray should have chosen such an out-of-the-way spot, but I knew him for a man of many whims.

The street, when I found it, turned out to be a respectable little place – boarding-houses and architects' offices, with a few antiquity shops, and a picture-cleaner's. The restaurant took some finding, for it was one of those discreet establishments, common enough in France, where no edibles are displayed in the British fashion, and muslin half-curtains deck the windows. Only the doormat, lettered with the proprietor's name, remained to guide the hungry.

I gave a waiter my hat and stick and was ushered into a garish dining-room, apparently full of people. A single violinist was discoursing music from beside the grill. The occupants were not quite the kind one expects to find in an eating-house in a side street. The men were all in evening dress with white waistcoats, and the women looked either *demi-mondaines* or those who follow their taste in clothes. Various eyes looked curiously at me as I entered. I guessed that the restaurant had, by one of those odd freaks of Londoners, become for a moment the fashion.

The proprietor met me half-way up the room. He might call himself Rapaccini, but he was obviously a German.

'Mr Geelvrai,' he nodded. 'He has engaged a private room. Vill you follow, sir?'

A narrow stairway broke into the wall on the left side of the dining-room. I followed the manager up it and along a short corridor to a door which filled its end. He ushered me into a brightly-lit little room where a table was laid for two.

'Mr Geelvrai comes often here,' said the manager. 'He vill be lat – sometimes. Everything is ready, sir. I hope you vill be pleased.'

It looked inviting enough, but the air smelt stuffy. Then I saw that, though the night was warm, the window was shut and the curtains drawn. I pulled back the curtains, and to my surprise saw that the shutters were closed.

'You must open these,' I said, 'or we'll stifle.'

The manager glanced at the window. 'I vill send a waiter,' he said, and departed. The door seemed to shut with an odd click.

I flung myself down in one of the arm-chairs, for I was feeling pretty tired. The little table beckoned alluringly, for I was also hungry. I remember there was a mass of pink roses on it. A bottle of champagne, with the cork loose, stood in a wine-cooler on the sideboard, and there was an unopened bottle beside it. It seemed to me that Macgillivray, when he dined here, did himself rather well.

The promised waiter did not arrive, and the stuffiness was making me very thirsty. I looked for a bell, but could not see one. My watch told me it was now a quarter to eight, but there was no sign of Macgillivray. I poured myself out a glass of champagne from the opened bottle, and was just about to drink it, when my eye caught something in a corner of the room.

It was one of those little mid-Victorian corner tables – I believe they call them 'what-nots' – which you will find in any boarding-house littered up with photographs and coral and 'Presents from Brighton'. On this one stood a photograph in a shabby frame, and I thought I recognised it.

I crossed the room and picked it up. It showed a man of thirty, with short side-whiskers, an ill-fitting jaw, and a drooping moustache. The duplicate of it was in Macgillivray's cabinet. It was Mr Routh, the ex-union leader.

There was nothing very remarkable about that after all, but it gave me a nasty shock. The room now seemed a sinister place, as well as intolerably close. There was still no sign of the waiter to open the window, so I thought I would wait for Macgillivray downstairs.

But the door would not open. The handle would not turn. It did not seem to be locked, but rather to have shut with some kind of patent spring. I noticed that the whole thing was a powerful piece of oak with a heavy framework, very unlike the usual flimsy restaurant doors.

My first instinct was to make a deuce of a row and attract the attention of the diners below. I own I was beginning to feel badly frightened. Clearly I had got into some sort of trap. Macgillivray's invitation might have been a hoax, for it is not difficult to counterfeit a man's voice on the telephone. With an effort I forced myself into calmness. It was preposterous to think that anything could happen to me in a room not thirty feet from where a score or two of ordinary citizens were dining. I had only to raise my voice to bring inquirers.

Yes, but above all things I did not want a row. It would never do for a rising lawyer and a Member of Parliament to be found shouting for help in an upper chamber of a Bloomsbury restaurant. The worst deductions would be drawn from the open bottle of champagne. Besides, it might be all right after all. The door might have got stuck. Macgillivray at that very moment might be on his way up.

So I sat down and waited. Then I remembered my thirst, and stretched out my hand to the glass of champagne.

But at that instant I looked towards the window, and set down the wine untasted.

It was a very odd window. The lower end was almost flush with the floor, and the hinges of the shutters seemed to be only on one side. As I stared I began to wonder whether it was a window at all.

Next moment my doubts were solved. The window swung open like a door, and in the dark cavity stood a man.

Strangely enough I knew him. His figure was not one that is readily forgotten.

'Good evening, Mr Docken,' I said; 'will you have a glass of champagne?'

A year before, on the South-Eastern Circuit, I had appeared for the defence in a burglary case. Criminal law was not my province, but now and then I took a case to keep my hand in, for it is the best training in the world for the handling of witnesses. This case had been peculiar. A certain Bill Docken was the accused, a gentleman who bore a bad reputation in the eyes of the police. The evidence against him was strong, but it was more or less tainted, being chiefly that of two former accomplices – a proof that there is small truth in the proverbial honour among thieves. It was an ugly business, and my sympathies were with the accused, for though he may very well have been guilty, yet he had been the victim of a shabby trick. Anyhow I put my back into the case, and after a hard struggle got a verdict of 'Not Guilty'. Mr Docken had been kind enough to express his appreciation of my efforts, and to ask in a hoarse whisper how I had 'squared the old bird', meaning the Judge. He did not understand the subtleties of the English law of evidence.

He shambled into the room, a huge hulking figure of a man, with the thickness of chest which under happier circumstances might have made him a terror in the prize-ring. His features wore a heavy scowl which slowly cleared to a flicker of recognition.

'By God, it's the lawyer-chap,' he muttered.

I pointed to the glass of champagne. 'I don't mind if I do,' he said. ''Ere's 'ealth!' He swallowed the wine at a gulp and wiped his mouth on his sleeve. ''Ave a drop yourself, guv'nor,' he added. 'A glass of bubbly will cheer you up.'

'Well, Mr Docken,' I said, 'I hope I see you fit.' I was getting wonderfully collected now that the suspense was over.

'Pretty fair, sir. Pretty fair. Able to do my day's work like an honest man.'

'And what brings you here?'

'A little job I'm on. Some friends of mine wants you out of the road for a bit and they've sent me to fetch you. It's a bit of luck for you that you've struck a friend. We needn't 'ave no unpleasantness, seein' we're both what you might call men of the world.'

'I appreciate the compliment,' I said. 'But where do you propose to take me?'

'Dunno. It's some lay near the Docks. I've got a motor-car waitin' at the back of the 'ouse.'

'But supposing I don't want to go?'

'My orders admits no excuse,' he said solemnly. 'You're a sensible chap, and can see that in a scrap I could down you easy.'

'Very likely,' I said. 'But, man, you must be mad to talk like that. Downstairs there is a dining-room full of people. I have only to lift my voice to bring the police.'

'You're a kid,' he said scornfully. 'Them geysers downstairs are all in the job. That was a flat-catching rig to get you up here so as you wouldn't suspect nothing. If you was to go down now – which you ain't going to be allowed to do – you wouldn't find a blamed soul in the place. I must say you're a bit softer than I 'oped after the 'andsome way you talked over yon old juggins with the wig at Maidstone.'

Mr Docken took the bottle from the wine-cooler and filled himself another glass.

It sounded horribly convincing. If I was to be kidnapped and smuggled away, Lumley would have scored half a success. Not the whole; for, as I swiftly reflected, I had put Felix on the track of Tuke, and there was every chance that Tommy and Pitt-Heron would be saved. But for myself it looked pretty black. The more my scheme succeeded the more likely the Power-House would be to wreak its vengeance on me once I was spirited from the open-air world into its dark labyrinths. I made a great effort to keep my voice even and calm.

'Mr Docken,' I said, 'I once did you a good turn. But for me you might be doing time now instead of drinking champagne like a gentleman. Your pals played you a pretty low trick and that was why I stuck out for you. I didn't think you were the kind of man to forget a friend.'

'No more I am,' said he. 'The man who says Bill Docken would go back on a pal is a liar.'

'Well, here's your chance to pay your debts. The men who employ you are my deadly enemies and want to do me in. I'm not a match for you. You're a stronger fellow and can drag me off and hand me over to them. But if you do I'm done with. Make no mistake about that. I put it to you as a decent fellow. Are you going to go back on the man who has been a good friend to you?'

He shifted from one foot to another with his eyes on the ceiling. He was obviously in difficulties. Then he tried another glass of champagne.

'I dursn't, guv'nor. I dursn't let you go. Them I work for would cut my throat as soon as look at me. Besides, it ain't no good. If I was to go off and leave you there'd be plenty more in this 'ouse as would do the job. You're up against it, guv'nor. But take a sensible view and come with me. They don't mean you no real 'arm. I'll take my Bible oath on it. Only to keep you quiet for a bit, for you've run across one of their games. They won't do you no 'urt if you speak 'em fair. Be a sport and take it smiling-like.'

'You're afraid of them,' I said.

'Yuss. I'm afraid. Black afraid. So would you be if you knew the gents. I'd rather take on the whole Rat Lane crowd – you know them as I mean – on a Saturday night when they're out for business than go back to my gents and say as 'ow I had shirked the job.'

He shivered. 'Good Lord, they'd freeze the 'eart out of a bull-pup.'

'You're afraid,' I said slowly. 'So you're going to give me up to the men you're afraid of to do as they like with me. I never expected it of you, Bill. I thought you were the kind of lad who would send any gang to the devil before you'd go back on a pal.'

'Don't say that,' he said almost plaintively. 'You don't 'alf know the 'ole I'm in.' His eye seemed to be wandering, and he yawned deeply.

Just then a great noise began below. I heard a voice speaking, a loud peremptory voice. Then my name was shouted: 'Leithen! Leithen! Are you there?'

There could be no mistaking that stout Yorkshire tongue. By some miracle Chapman had followed me and was raising Cain downstairs.

My heart leaped with the sudden revulsion. 'I'm here,' I yelled. 'Upstairs. Come up and let me out!'

Then I turned with a smile of triumph to Bill.

'My friends have come,' I said. 'You're too late for the job. Get back and tell your masters that.'

He was swaying on his feet, and he suddenly lurched

towards me. 'You come along. By God, you think you've done me. I'll let you see.'

His voice was growing thick and he stopped short. 'What the 'ell's wrong with me?' he gasped. 'I'm goin' all queer.'

He was like a man far gone in liquor, but three glasses of champagne would never have touched a head like Bill's. I saw what was up with him. He was not drunk, but drugged.

'They've doped the wine,' I cried. 'They put it there for me to drink it and go to sleep.'

There is always something which is the last straw to any man. You may insult and outrage him and he will bear it patiently, but touch the quick in his temper and he will turn. Apparently for Bill drugging was the unforgivable sin. His eye lost for a moment its confusion. He squared his shoulders and roared like a bull.

'Doped, by God!' he cried. 'Who done it?'

'The men who shut me in this room. Burst that door and you will find them.'

He turned a blazing face on the locked door and hurled his huge weight on it. It cracked and bent, but the lock and hinges held. I could see that sleep was overwhelming him and that his limbs were stiffening, but his anger was still strong enough for another effort. Again he drew himself together like a big cat and flung himself on the woodwork. The hinges tore from the jambs and the whole outfit fell forward into the passage in a cloud of splinters and dust and broken plaster.

It was Mr Docken's final effort. He lay on the top of the wreckage he had made, like Samson among the ruins of Gaza, a senseless and slumbering hulk.

I picked up the unopened bottle of champagne – it was the

only weapon available – and stepped over his body. I was beginning to enjoy myself amazingly.

As I expected, there was a man in the corridor, a little fellow in waiter's clothes with a tweed jacket instead of a dress-coat. If he had a pistol I knew I was done, but I gambled upon the disinclination of the management for the sound of shooting.

He had a knife, but he never had a chance to use it. My champagne bottle descended on his head and he dropped like a log.

There were men coming upstairs – not Chapman, for I still heard his hoarse shouts in the dining-room. If they once got up they could force me back through that hideous room by the door through which Docken had come, and in five minutes I should be in their motor-car.

There was only one thing to do. I jumped from the stair-head right down among them. I think there were three, and my descent toppled them over. We rolled in a wild whirling mass and cascaded into the dining-room, where my head bumped violently on the parquet.

I expected a bit of a grapple, but none came. My wits were pretty woolly, but I managed to scramble to my feet. The heels of my enemies were disappearing up the staircase. Chapman was pawing my ribs to discover if there were any bones broken. There was not another soul in the room except two policemen who were pushing their way in from the street. Chapman was flushed and breathing heavily: his coat had a big split down the seams at the shoulder, but his face was happy as a child's.

I caught his arm and spoke in his ear. 'We've got to get out of this at once. How can we square these policemen? There must be no inquiry and nothing in the papers. Do you hear?'

'That's all right,' said Chapman. 'These bobbies are friends of mine, two good lads from Wensleydale. On my road here I told them to give me a bit of law and follow me, for I thought they might be wanted. They didn't come too soon to spoil sport, for I've been knocking furriners about for ten minutes. You seem to have been putting up a tidy scrap yourself.'

'Let's get home first,' I said, for I was beginning to think of the bigger thing.

I wrote a chit for Macgillivray which I asked one of the constables to take to Scotland Yard. It was to beg that nothing should be done yet in the business of the restaurant, and above all, that nothing should get into the papers. Then I asked the other to see us home. It was a queer request for two able-bodied men to make on a summer evening in the busiest part of London, but I was taking no chances. The Power-House had declared war on me, and I knew it would be war without quarter.

I was in a fever to get out of that place. My momentary lust of battle had gone, and every stone of that building seemed to me a threat. Chapman would have liked to spend a happy hour rummaging through the house, but the gravity of my face persuaded him. The truth is, I was bewildered. I could not understand the reason of this sudden attack. Lumley's spies must long ago have told him enough to connect me with the Bokhara business. My visits to the Embassy alone were proof enough. But now he must have found something new, something which startled him, or else there had been wild doings in Turkestan.

I won't forget that walk home in a hurry. It was a fine July twilight. The streets were full of the usual crowd, shop-girls in thin frocks, promenading clerks, and all the flotsam of a London summer. You would have said it was the safest place on earth. But I was glad we had the policeman with us, who at the end of one beat passed us on to his colleague, and I was glad of Chapman. For I am morally certain I would never have got home alone.

The queer thing is that there was no sign of trouble till we got into Oxford Street. Then I became aware that there were people on these pavements who knew all about me. I first noticed it at the mouth of one of those little dark side-alleys which run up into mews and small dingy courts. I found myself being skilfully edged away from Chapman into the shadow, but I noticed it in time and butted my way back to the pavement. I couldn't make out who the people were who hustled me. They seemed nondescripts of all sorts, but I fancied there were women among them.

This happened twice, and I got wary, but I was nearly caught before we reached Oxford Circus. There was a front of a big shop rebuilding, and the usual wooden barricade with a gate. Just as we passed it there was a special throng on the pavement, and I, being next the wall, got pushed against the gate. Suddenly it gave, and I was pressed inward. I was right inside before I realised my danger, and the gate was closing. There must have been people there, but I could see nothing in the gloom.

It was no time for false pride. I yelled to Chapman, and the next second his burly shoulder was in the gap. The hustlers vanished, and I seemed to hear a polite voice begging my pardon.

After that Chapman and I linked arms and struck across Mayfair. But I did not feel safe till I was in the flat with the door bolted.

We had a long drink, and I stretched myself in an armchair, for I was as tired as if I had come out of a big game of Rugby football.

'I owe you a good deal, old man,' I said. 'I think I'll join the Labour Party. You can tell your fellows to send me their whips. What possessed you to come to look for me?'

The explanation was simple. I had mentioned the restaurant in my telephone message, and the name had awakened a recollection in Chapman's mind. He could not fix it at first, but by-and-by he remembered that the place had cropped up in the Routh case. Routh's London headquarters had been at the restaurant in Antioch Street. As soon as he remembered this he got into a taxi and descended at the corner of the street, where by sheer luck he fell in with his Wensleydale friends.

He said he had marched into the restaurant and found it empty, but for an ill-favoured manager, who denied all knowledge of me. Then, fortunately, he chose to make certain by shouting my name, and heard my answer. After that he knocked the manager down, and was presently assaulted by several men whom he described as 'furrin muck'. They had knives, of which he made very little, for he seems to have swung a table as a battering-ram and left sore limbs behind him.

He was on the top of his form. 'I haven't enjoyed anything so much since I was a lad at school,' he informed me. 'I was beginning to think your Power-House was a wash-out, but Lord! it's been busy enough tonight. This is what I call life!'

My spirits could not keep pace with his. The truth is that I was miserably puzzled – not afraid so much as mystified. I couldn't make out this sudden dead-set at me. Either they knew more than I bargained for, or I knew far too little.

'It's all very well,' I said, 'but I don't see how this is going to end. We can't keep up the pace long. At this rate it will be only a matter of hours till they get me.'

We pretty well barricaded ourselves in the flat, and, at his earnest request, I restored to Chapman his revolver.

Then I got the clue I had been longing for. It was about eleven o'clock, while we were sitting smoking, when the telephone bell rang. It was Felix who spoke.

'I have news for you,' he said. 'The hunters have met the hunted, and one of the hunters is dead. The other is a prisoner in our hands. He has confessed.'

It had been black murder in intent. The frontier police had shadowed the two men into the cup of a glen, where they met Tommy and Pitt-Heron. The four had spoken together for a little, and then Tuke had fired deliberately at Charles and had grazed his ear. Whereupon Tommy had charged him and knocked the pistol from his hand. The assailant had fled, but a long shot from the police on the hillside had toppled him over. Tommy had felled Saronov with his fists, and the man had abjectly surrendered. He had confessed, Felix said, but what the confession was he did not know.

SEVEN

I Find Sanctuary

My nervousness and indecision dropped from me at the news. I had won the first round, and I would win the last, for it suddenly became clear to me that I had now evidence which would blast Lumley. I believed that it would not be hard to prove his identity with Pavia and his receipt of the telegram from Saronov; Tuke was his creature, and Tuke's murderous mission was his doing. No doubt I knew little and could prove nothing about the big thing, the Power-House, but conspiracy to murder is not the lightest of criminal charges. I was beginning to see my way to checkmating my friend, at least so far as Pitt-Heron was concerned. Provided – and it was a pretty big proviso – that he gave me the chance to use my knowledge.

That, I foresaw, was going to be the difficulty. What I knew now Lumley had known hours before. The reason of the affair at Antioch Street was now only too clear. If he believed that I had damning evidence against him – and there was no doubt he suspected it – then he would do his best to stop my mouth. I must get my statement lodged in the proper quarter at the earliest possible moment.

The next twenty-four hours, I feared, were going to be too sensational for comfort. And yet I cannot say that I was afraid. I was too full of pride to be in a funk. I had lost my awe of Lumley through scoring a point against him. Had I known more I should have been less at my ease. It was this confidence which prevented me doing the obvious safe thing – ringing up Macgillivray, telling him the gist of my story, and getting him to put me under police protection. I thought I was clever enough to see the thing through myself. And it must have been the same over-confidence which prevented Lumley getting at me that night. An organisation like his could easily have got into the flat and done for us both. I suppose the explanation is that he did not yet know how much I knew, and was not ready to take the last steps in silencing me.

I sat up till the small hours, marshalling my evidence in a formal statement and making two copies of it. One was destined for Macgillivray and the other for Felix, for I was taking no risks. I went to bed and slept peacefully, and was awakened as usual by Waters. My man slept out, and used to turn up in the morning about seven. It was all so normal and homely that I could have believed my adventures of the night before a dream. In the summer sunlight the ways of darkness seemed very distant. I dressed in excellent spirits and made a hearty breakfast.

Then I gave the docile Chapman his instructions. He must take the document to Scotland Yard, ask to see Macgillivray, and put it into his hands. Then he must ring me up at once at Down Street and tell me that he had done this. I had already telephoned to my clerk that I would not be at the Temple that day. It seems a simple thing to travel less than a mile in the most frequented part of London in broad daylight and perform an easy act like carrying a letter; but I knew that Lumley's spies would be active, and would connect Chapman sufficiently with me to think him worth following. In that case there might be an attempt at violence. I thought it my duty to tell him this, but he laughed me to scorn. He proposed to walk, and he begged to be shown the man who would meddle with him. Chapman, after last night, was prepared to take on all comers. He put my letter to Macgillivray in his inner pocket, buttoned his coat, crushed down his felt hat on his head, and defiantly set forth.

I expected a message from him in half an hour, for he was a rapid walker. But the half-hour passed, then the three-quarters, and nothing happened. At eleven I rang up Scotland Yard, but they had no news of him.

Then I became miserably anxious, for it was clear that some disaster had overtaken my messenger. My first impulse was to set out myself to look for him, but a moment's reflection convinced me that that would be playing into the enemy's hands. For an hour I wrestled with my impatience, and then a few minutes after twelve I was rung up by St Thomas's Hospital.

A young doctor spoke, and said that Mr Chapman had asked him to tell me what had happened. He had been run down by a motor-car at the corner of Whitehall, nothing serious – only a bad shake and some scalp wounds. In a day or so he would be able to leave.

Then he added what drove the blood from my heart. 'Mr Chapman personally wished me to tell you,' he said, 'that the letter has gone.' I stammered some reply asking his meaning. 'He said he thinks,' I was told, 'that, while he was being assisted to his feet, his pocket was picked and a letter taken. He said you would know what he meant.'

I knew only too well what he meant. Lumley had got my statement, and realised precisely how much I knew and what was the weight of evidence against him. Before he had only suspected, now he knew. He must know, too, that there would be a copy somewhere which I would try to deliver. It was going to be harder than I had fancied to get my news to the proper ears, and I had to anticipate the extreme of violence on the part of my opponents.

The thought of the peril restored my coolness. I locked the outer door of my flat, and telephoned to the garage where I kept my car, bidding Stagg call for me at two o'clock precisely. Then I lit a pipe and strove to banish the whole business from my thoughts, for fussing would do me no good.

Presently it occurred to me to ring up Felix and give him some notion of the position. But I found that my telephone was now broken and connection was impossible. The spoken as well as the written word was to be denied me. That had happened in the last half-hour, and I didn't believe it was by accident. Also my man Waters, whom I had sent out on an errand after breakfast, had never returned. The state of siege had begun.

It was a blazing hot midsummer day. The water-carts were sprinkling Piccadilly, and looking from my window I could see leisurely and elegant gentlemen taking their morning stroll. A florist's cart full of roses stood below me in the street. The summer smell of town – a mixture of tar, flowers, dust, and patchouli – rose in gusts through the hot air. It was the homely London I knew so well, and I was somehow an exile from it. I was being shepherded into a dismal isolation, which, unless I won help, might mean death. I was cool enough now, but I will not deny that I was miserably anxious. I cursed my false confidence the night before. By now I might have had Macgillivray and his men by my side. As it was, I wondered if I should ever see them.

I changed into a flannel suit, lunched off sandwiches and a

whisky-and-soda, and at two o'clock looked for Stagg and my car. He was five minutes late, a thing which had never happened before. But I never welcomed anything so gladly as the sight of that car. I had hardly dared to hope that it would reach me.

My goal was the Embassy in Belgrave Square, but I was convinced that if I approached it directly I should share the fate of Chapman. Worse, for from me they would not merely snatch the letter. What I had once written I could write again, and if they wished to ensure my silence it must be by more drastic methods. I proposed to baffle my pursuers by taking a wide circuit round the western suburbs of London, returning to the Embassy when I thought the coast clear.

It was a tremendous relief to go down the stairs and emerge into the hot daylight. I gave Stagg his instructions, and lay back in the closed car with a curious fluttering sense of anticipation. I had begun the last round in a wild game. There was a man at the corner of Down Street who seemed to peer curiously at the car. He was doubtless one of my watchers.

We went up Park Lane into the Edgware Road, my instructions to Stagg being to make a circuit by Harrow and Brentford. Now that I was ensconced in my car I felt a trifle safer, and my tense nerves relaxed. I grew drowsy and allowed myself to sink into a half doze. The stolid back of Stagg filled my gaze, as it had filled it a fortnight ago on the western road, and I admired lazily the brick-red of his neck. He had been in the Guards, and a Boer bullet at Modder River had left a long scar at the nape of his neck, which gave to his hair the appearance of being badly cut. He had told me the story on Exmoor.

Suddenly I rubbed my eyes. There was no scar there; the

hair of the chauffeur grew regularly down to his coat-collar. The resemblance had been perfect, the voice was Stagg's, but clearly it was not Stagg who now drove my car.

I pulled the blind down over the front window as if to shelter myself from the sun. Looking out, I saw that we were some distance up the Edgware Road, nearing the point where the Marylebone Road joins it. Now or never was my chance, for at the corner there is always a block in the traffic.

The car slowed down in obedience to a policeman's up-lifted hand, and very gently I opened the door on the left side. Since the car was new it opened softly, and in two seconds I had stepped out, shut it again, and made a dive between a butcher's cart and a motor-bus for the side-walk. I gave one glance back and saw the unconscious chauffeur still rigid at the wheel.

I dodged unobtrusively through the crowd on the pavement, with my hand on my breast-pocket to see that my paper was still there. There was a little picture-shop near by to which I used to go occasionally, owned by a man who was an adept at cleaning and restoring. I had sent him customers and he was likely to prove a friend. So I dived into his doorway, which made a cool pit of shade after the glaring street, and found him, spectacles on nose, busy examining some dusty prints.

He greeted me cordially and followed me into the back shop.

'Mr Levison,' I said, 'have you a back door?'

He looked at me in some surprise. 'Why, yes; there is the door into the lane which runs from Edgeley Street into Connaught Mews.'

'Will you let me use it? There is a friend outside whom I wish to avoid. Such things happen, you know.'

He smiled comprehendingly. 'Certainly, sir. Come this way.' And he led me through a dark passage hung with dingy Old Masters to a little yard filled with the debris of picture frames. There he unlocked a door in the wall and I found myself in a narrow alley. As I emerged I heard the bell of the shop-door ring. 'If any one inquires, you have not seen me here, remember,' I said, and Mr Levison nodded. He was an artist in his small way and liked the scent of a mystery.

I ran down the lane and by various cross streets made my way into Bayswater. I believed that I had thrown my trackers for the moment off the scent, but I had got to get to the Embassy, and that neighbourhood was sure to be closely watched. I came out on the Bayswater Road pretty far west, and resolved to strike south-east across the Park. My reason was that the neighbourhood of Hyde Park Corner was certain at that time of day to be pretty well crowded, and I felt more security in a throng than in the empty streets of Kensington. Now that I come to think of it, it was a rash thing to do, for since Lumley knew the full extent of my knowledge, he was likely to deal more violently with me than with Chapman, and the seclusion of the Park offered him too good a chance.

I crossed the riding-track, and struck over the open space where the Sunday demonstrations are held. There was nothing there but nurses and perambulators, children at play, and dogs being exercised. Presently I reached Grosvenor Gate, where on the little green chairs well-dressed people were taking the air. I recognised several acquaintances, and stopped for a moment to talk to one of them. Then I emerged in Park Lane, and walked down it to Hamilton Place.

So far I thought I had not been followed, but now once more I had the indefinable but unerring sensation of being watched. I caught a man looking eagerly at me from the other side of the street, and it seemed to me that he made a sign to some one farther off. There was now less than a quarter of a mile between me and Belgrave Square, but I saw that it would be a hard course to cover.

Once in Piccadilly, there could be no doubt about my watchers. Lumley was doing the thing in style this time. Last night it had only been a trial trip, but now the whole energies of the Power-House were on the job. The place was filled with the usual mid-season crowd, and I had to take off my hat several times. Up in the bow-window of the Bachelors' Club a young friend of mine was writing a letter and sipping a long drink with an air of profound boredom. I would have given much for his *ennui*, for my life at the moment was painfully exciting. I was alone in that crowd, isolated and proscribed, and there was no help save in my own wits. If I spoke to a policeman he would think me drunk or mad, and yet I was on the edge of being made the victim of a far subtler crime than fell within the purview of the Metropolitan force.

Now I saw how thin is the protection of civilisation. An accident and a bogus ambulance, false charge and a bogus arrest – there were a dozen ways of spiriting me out of this gay, bustling world. I foresaw that, if I delayed, my nerve would break, so I boldly set off across the road.

I jolly nearly shared the fate of Chapman. A car which seemed about to draw up at a club door suddenly swerved across the street, and I had to dash to an island to escape it. It was no occasion to hesitate, so, dodging a bus and missing a motor-bicycle by a hair's breadth, I rushed across the remaining distance and reached the railings of the Green Park.

Here there were fewer people, and several queer things began to happen. A little group of workmen with their tools were standing by the kerb, and they suddenly moved towards me. A pavement artist, who looked like a cripple, scrambled to his feet and moved in the same direction. There was a policeman at the corner, and I saw a well-dressed man go up to him, say something and nod in my direction, and the policeman too began to move towards me.

I did not await them. I took to my heels and ran for my life down Grosvenor Place.

Long ago at Eton I had won the school mile, and at Oxford I was a second string for the quarter. But never at Eton or at Oxford did I run as I ran then. It was blisteringly hot, but I did not feel it, for my hands were clammy and my heart felt like a cold stone. I do not know how the pursuit got on, for I did not think of it. I did not reflect what kind of spectacle I must afford running like a thief in a London thoroughfare on a June afternoon. I only knew that my enemies were around and behind me, and that in front, a few hundred yards away, lay safety.

But even as I ran I had the sense to think out my movements, and to realise that the front door of the Embassy was impossible. For one thing, it would be watched, and for another, before the solemn footmen opened it, my pursuers would be upon me. My only hope was the back door.

I twisted into the Mews behind the north side of the Square, and as I turned I saw two men run up from the Square as if to cut me off. A whistle was blown, and more men appeared – one entering from the far end of the Mews, one darting from a public-house door, and one sliding down a ladder from a stable-loft. This last was nearest me, and tried to trip me, but I rejoice to say that a left-hander on the chin sent him sprawling on the cobbles. I remembered that the Embassy was the fifth house from the end, and feverishly I tried to count the houses by their backs. It is not so easy as it sounds, for the modern London householder studs his back premises with excrescences which seem to melt into his neighbour's. In the end I had to make a guess at the door, which, to my joy, was unlocked. I rushed in and banged it behind me.

I found myself in a stone passage, with on one side a door opening on a garage. There was a wooden staircase leading to an upper floor, and a glass door in front, which opened into a large disused room full of boxes. Beyond were two doors, one of which was locked. The other abutted on a steep iron stairway, which obviously led to the lower regions of the house.

I ran down the stair – it was no more than a ladder – crossed a small courtyard, traversed a passage, and burst into the kitchen, where I confronted an astonished white-capped chef in the act of lifting a pot from the fire.

His face was red and wrathful, and I thought that he was going to fling the pot at my head. I had disturbed him in some delicate operation, and his artist's pride was outraged.

'Monsieur,' I stammered in French, 'I seek your pardon for my intrusion. There were circumstances which compelled me to enter this house by the back premises. I am an acquaintance of his Excellency, your patron, and an old friend of Monsieur Felix. I beg you of your kindness to direct me to Monsieur Felix's room, or to bid someone take me there.'

My abject apologies mollified him.

'It is a grave offence, monsieur,' he said, 'an unparalleled offence, to enter my kitchen at this hour. I fear you have irremediably spoiled the new casserole dish that I was endeavouring to compose.'

I was ready to go on my knees to the offended artist.

'It grieves me indeed to have interfered with so rare an art, which I have often admired at his Excellency's table. But there is danger behind me, and an urgent mission in front. Monsieur will forgive me? Necessity will sometimes overrule the finest sensibility.'

He bowed to me, and I bowed to him, and my pardon was assured.

Suddenly a door opened, another than that by which I had entered, and a man appeared whom I took to be a footman. He was struggling into his livery coat, but at the sight of me he dropped it. I thought I recognised the face as that of the man who had emerged from the public-house and tried to cut me off.

' 'Ere, Mister Alphonse,' he cried, ' 'elp me to collar this man. The police are after 'im.'

'You forget, my friend,' I said, 'that an Embassy is privileged ground which the police can't enter. I desire to be taken before his Excellency.'

'So that's yer game,' he shouted. 'But two can play at that. 'Ere, give me an 'and, moosoo, and we'll 'ave him in the street in a jiffy. There's two 'undred of the best in our pockets if we 'ands 'im over to them as wants 'im.'

The cook looked puzzled and a little frightened.

'Will you allow them to outrage your kitchen – an Embassy kitchen, too – without your consent?' I said.

'What have you done?' he asked in French.

'Only what your patron will approve,' I replied in the same tongue. '*Messieurs les assassins* have a grudge against me.'

He still hesitated, while the young footman advanced on me. He was fingering something in his trousers-pocket which I did not like.

Now was the time when, as they say in America, I should have got busy with my gun; but alas! I had no gun. I feared supports for the enemy, for the footman at the first sight of me had run back the way he had come, and I had heard a low whistle.

What might have happened I do not know, had not the god appeared from the machine in the person of Hewins, the butler.

'Hewins,' I said, 'you know me. I have often dined here, and you know that I am a friend of Monsieur Felix. I am on my way to see him on an urgent matter, and for various reasons I had to enter by Monsieur Alphonse's kitchen. Will you take me at once to Monsieur Felix?'

Hewins bowed, and on his imperturbable face there appeared no sign of surprise. 'This way, sir,' was all he said.

As I followed him I saw the footman plucking nervously at the something in his trousers-pocket. Lumley's agents apparently had not always the courage to follow his instructions to the letter, for I made no doubt that the order had been to take me alive or dead.

I found Felix alone, and flung myself into an armchair.

'My dear chap,' I said, 'take my advice and advise His Excellency to sack the red-haired footman.'

From that moment I date that sense of mastery over a situation which drives out fear. I had been living for weeks under a dark pall, and suddenly the skies had lightened. I had found sanctuary. Whatever happened to me now the worst was past, for I had done my job.

Felix was looking at me curiously, for, jaded, scarlet, dishevelled, I was an odd figure for a London afternoon. 'Things seem to have been marching fast with you,' he said.

'They have, but I think the march is over. I want to ask several favours. First, here is a document which sets out certain facts. I shall ring up Macgillivray at Scotland Yard and ask him to come here at nine thirty this evening. When he

comes I want you to give him this and ask him to read it at
once. He will know how to act on it.'

Felix nodded. 'And the next?'

'Give me a telegraph form. I want a wire sent at once by
someone who can be trusted.' He handed me a form and I
wrote out a telegram to Lumley at the Albany, saying that I
proposed to call upon him that evening at eight sharp, and
asking him to receive me.

'Next?' said Felix.

'Next and last, I want a room with a door which will lock, a
hot bath, and something to eat about seven. I might be
permitted to taste Monsieur Alphonse's new casserole dish.'

I rang up Macgillivray, reminded him of his promise, and
told him what awaited him at nine thirty. Then I had a wash,
and afterwards at my leisure gave Felix a sketch of the day's
doings. I have never felt more completely at my ease, for
whatever happened I was certain that I had spoiled Lumley's
game. He would know by now that I had reached the
Embassy, and that any further attempts on my life and liberty
were futile. My telegram would show him that I was prepared
to offer terms, and I would certainly be permitted to reach the
Albany unmolested. To the meeting with my adversary I
looked forward without qualms, but with the most lively
interest. I had my own theories about that distinguished
criminal, and I hoped to bring them to the proof.

Just before seven I had a reply to my wire. Mr Lumley said
he would be delighted to see me. The telegram was directed
to me at the Embassy, though I had put no address on the one
I sent. Lumley, of course, knew all my movements. I could
picture him sitting in his chair, like some Chief of Staff,
receiving every few minutes the reports of his agents. All the
same, Napoleon had fought his Waterloo.

EIGHT

The Power-House

I left Belgrave Square about a quarter to eight and retraced my steps along the route which for me that afternoon had been so full of tremors. I was still being watched – a little observation told me that – but I would not be interfered with, provided my way lay in a certain direction. So completely without nervousness was I that at the top of Constitution Hill I struck into the Green Park and kept to the grass till I emerged into Piccadilly opposite Devonshire House. A light wind had risen, and the evening had grown pleasantly cool. I met several men I knew going out to dinner on foot, and stopped to exchange greetings. From my clothes they thought I had just returned from a day in the country.

I reached the Albany as the clock was striking eight. Lumley's rooms were on the first floor, and I was evidently expected, for the porter himself conducted me to them and waited by me till the door was opened by a manservant.

You know those rococo, late Georgian, Albany rooms, large, square, clumsily corniced. Lumley's was lined with books, which I saw at a glance were of a different type from those in his working library at his country house. This was the collection of a bibliophile, and in the light of the summer evening the rows of tall volumes in vellum and morocco lined the walls like some rich tapestry.

The valet retired and shut the door, and presently from a

little inner chamber came his master. He was dressed for dinner, and wore more than ever the air of the eminent diplomat. Again I had the old feeling of incredulity. It was the Lumley I had met two nights before at dinner, the friend of Viceroys and Cabinet Ministers. It was hard to connect him with Antioch Street or the red-haired footman with a pistol. Or with Tuke? Yes, I decided, Tuke fitted into the frame. Both were brains cut loose from the decencies that make life possible.

'Good evening, Mr Leithen,' he said pleasantly. 'As you have fixed the hour of eight, may I offer you dinner?'

'Thank you,' I replied, 'but I have already dined. I have chosen an awkward time, but my business need not take long.'

'So?' he said. 'I am always glad to see you at any hour.'

'And I prefer to see the master rather than the subordinates who have been infesting my life during the past week.'

We both laughed. 'I am afraid you have had some annoyance, Mr Leithen,' he said. 'But remember, I gave you fair warning.'

'True. And I have come to do the same kindness to you. That part of the game, at any rate, is over.'

'Over?' he queried, raising his eyebrows.

'Yes, over,' I said, and took out my watch. 'Let us be quite frank with each other, Mr Lumley. There is really very little time to waste. As you have doubtless read the paper which you stole from my friend this morning, you know more or less the extent of my information.'

'Let us have frankness by all means. Yes, I have read your paper. A very creditable piece of work, if I may say so. You will rise in your profession, Mr Leithen. But surely you must realise that it carries you a very little way.'

'In a sense you are right. I am not in a position to reveal the full extent of your misdeeds. Of the Power-House and its doings I can only guess. But Pitt-Heron is on his way home, and he will be carefully safeguarded on that journey. Your creature, Saronov, has confessed. We shall know more very soon, and meantime I have clear evidence which implicates you in a conspiracy to murder.'

He did not answer, but I wished I could see behind his tinted spectacles to the look in his eyes. I think he had not been quite prepared for the line I took.

'I need not tell you, as a lawyer, Mr Leithen,' he said at last, 'that what seems good evidence on paper is often feeble enough in Court. You cannot suppose that I will tamely plead guilty to your charges. On the contrary, I will fight them with all the force that brains and money can give. You are an ingenious young man, but you are not the brightest jewel of the English Bar.'

'That also is true. I do not deny that some of my evidence may be weakened at the trial. It is even conceivable that you may be acquitted on some technical doubt. But you have forgotten one thing. From the day you leave the Court you will be a suspected man. The police of all Europe will be on your trail. You have been highly successful in the past, and why? Because you have been above suspicion, an honourable and distinguished gentleman, belonging to the best clubs, counting as your acquaintances the flower of our society. Now you will be a suspect, a man with a past, a centre of strange stories. I put it to you – how far are you likely to succeed under these conditions?'

He laughed.

'You have a talent for character-drawing, my friend. What makes you think I can work only if I live in the limelight of popularity?'

'The talent you mention,' I said. 'As I read your character –
and I think I am right – you are an artist in crime. You are not
the common cut-throat who acts out of passion or greed. No,
I think you are something subtler than that. You love power,
hidden power. You flatter your vanity by despising mankind
and making them your tools. You scorn the smattering of
inaccuracies which passes for human knowledge, and I will
not venture to say you are wrong. Therefore, you use your
brains to frustrate it. Unhappily the life of millions is built on
that smattering, so you are a foe to society. But there would
be no flavour in controlling subterranean things if you were
yourself a mole working in the dark. To get the full flavour,
the irony of it all, you must live in the light. I can imagine you
laughing in your soul as you move about our world, praising
it with your lips, patting it with your hands, and kicking its
props away with your feet. I can see the charm of it. But it is
over now.'

'Over?' he asked.

'Over,' I repeated. 'The end has come, the utter, final, and
absolute end.'

He made a sudden, odd, nervous movement, pushing his
glasses close back upon his eyes.

'What about yourself?' he said hoarsely. 'Do you think you
can play against me without suffering desperate penalties?'

He was holding a cord in his hand with a knob on the end
of it. He now touched a button in the knob, and there came
the faint sound of a bell.

The door was behind me, and he was looking beyond me
towards it. I was entirely at his mercy, but I never budged an
inch. I do not know how I managed to keep calm, but I did it,
and without much effort. I went on speaking, conscious that
the door had opened and that some one was behind me.

'It is really quite useless trying to frighten me. I am safe, because I am dealing with an intelligent man, and not with the ordinary half-witted criminal. You do not want my life in silly revenge. If you call in your man and strangle me between you what earthly good would it do you?'

He was looking beyond me, and the passion – a sudden white-hot passion like an epilepsy – was dying out of his face.

'A mistake, James,' he said. 'You can go.'

The door closed softly at my back.

'Yes. A mistake. I have a considerable admiration for you, Mr Lumley, and should be sorry to be disappointed.'

He laughed quite like an ordinary mortal. 'I am glad this affair is to be conducted on a basis of mutual respect. Now that the melodramatic overture is finished let us get to the business.'

'By all means,' I said. 'I promised to deal with you frankly. Well, let me put my last cards on the table. At half-past nine precisely the duplicate of that statement of mine which you annexed this morning will be handed to Scotland Yard. I may add that the authorities there know me, and are proceeding under my advice. When they read that statement they will act on it. You have therefore about one hour and a half, or say one and three-quarters, to make up your mind. You can still secure your freedom, but it must be elsewhere than in England.'

He had risen to his feet, and was pacing up and down the room.

'Will you oblige me by telling me one thing,' he said. 'If you believe me to be, as you say, a dangerous criminal, how do you reconcile it with your conscience to give me a chance of escape? It is your duty to bring me to justice.'

'I will tell you why,' I said. 'I, too, have a weak joint in my armour. Yours is that you can only succeed under the disguise of high respectability. That disguise, in any case, will be stripped from you. Mine is Pitt-Heron. I do not know how far he has entangled himself with you, but I know something of his weakness, and I don't want his career ruined and his wife's heart broken. He has learned his lesson, and will never mention you and your schemes to a mortal soul. Indeed, if I can help it, he will never know that any one shares his secret. The price of the chance of escape I offer you is that Pitt-Heron's past be buried for ever.'

He did not answer. He had his arms folded, walking up and down the room, and suddenly seemed to have aged enormously. I had the impression that I was dealing with a very old man.

'Mr Leithen,' he said at last, 'you are bold. You have a frankness which almost amounts to genius. You are wasted in your stupid profession, but your speculative powers are not equal to your other endowments, so you will probably remain in it, deterred by an illogical scruple from following your true bent. Your true *métier*, believe me, is what shallow people call crime. Speaking "without prejudice", as the idiot solicitors say, it would appear that we have both weak spots in our cases. Mine, you say, is that I can only work by using the conventions of what we agreed to call the machine. There may be truth in that. Yours is that you have a friend who lacks your iron-clad discretion. You offer a plan which saves both our weaknesses. By the way, what is it?'

I looked at my watch again. 'You have ample time to catch the night express to Paris.'

'And if not?'

'Then I am afraid there may be trouble with the police between ten and eleven o'clock.'

'Which, for all our sakes, would be a pity. Do you know you interest me uncommonly, for you confirm the accuracy of my judgment. I have always had a notion that some day I should run across, to my sorrow, just such a man as you. A man of very great intellectual power I can deal with, for that kind of brain is usually combined with the sort of high-strung imagination on which I can work. The same with your over-imaginative man. Yes, Pitt-Heron was of that type. Ordinary brains do not trouble me, for I puzzle them. Now, you are a man of good commonplace intelligence. Pray forgive the lukewarmness of the phrase; it is really a high compliment, for I am an austere critic. If you were that and no more you would not have succeeded. But you possess also a quite irrelevant gift of imagination. Not enough to upset your balance, but enough to do what your mere lawyer's talent could never have done. You have achieved a feat which is given to few – you have partially understood me. Believe me, I rate you high. You are the kind of foursquare being bedded in the concrete of our civilisation, on whom I have always felt I might some day come to grief . . . No, no, I am not trying to wheedle you. If I thought I could do that I should be sorry, for my discernment would have been at fault.'

'I warn you,' I said, 'that you are wasting precious time.'

He laughed quite cheerfully. 'I believe you are really anxious about my interests,' he said. 'That is a triumph indeed. Do you know, Mr Leithen, it is a mere whimsy of fate that you are not my disciple. If we had met earlier, and under other circumstances, I should have captured you. It is because you have in you a capacity for discipleship that you have succeeded in your opposition.'

'I abominate you and all your works,' I said, 'but I admire your courage.'

He shook his head gently.

'It is the wrong word. I am not courageous. To be brave means that you have conquered fear, but I have never had any fear to conquer. Believe me, Mr Leithen, I am quite impervious to threats. You come to me tonight and hold a pistol to my head. You offer me two alternatives, both of which mean failure. But how do you know that I regard them as failure? I have had what they call a good run for my money. No man since Napoleon has tasted such power. I may be willing to end it. Age creeps on and power may grow burdensome. I have always sat loose from common ambitions and common affections. For all you know I may regard you as a benefactor.'

All this talk looks futile when it is written down, but it was skilful enough, for it was taking every atom of exhilaration out of my victory. It was not idle brag. Every syllable rang true, as I knew in my bones. I felt myself in the presence of something enormously big, as if a small barbarian was desecrating the colossal Zeus of Pheidias with a coal hammer. But I also felt it inhuman and I hated it, and I clung to that hatred.

'You fear nothing and you believe nothing,' I said. 'Man, you should never have been allowed to live.'

He raised a deprecating hand. 'I am a sceptic about most things,' he said, 'but, believe me, I have my own worship. I venerate the intellect of man. I believe in its undreamed-of possibilities, when it grows free like an oak in the forest and is not dwarfed in a flower-pot. From that allegiance I have never wavered. That is the God I have never forsworn.'

I took out my watch.

'Permit me again to remind you that time presses.'

'True,' he said, smiling. 'The continental express will not

wait upon my confession. Your plan is certainly conceivable. There may be other and easier ways. I am not certain. I must think. Perhaps it would be wiser if you left me now, Mr Leithen. If I take your advice there will be various things to do. In any case there will be much to do.'

He led me to the door as if he were an ordinary host speeding an ordinary guest. I remember that on my way he pointed out a set of Aldines and called my attention to their beauty. He shook hands quite cordially and remarked on the fineness of the weather. That was the last I saw of this amazing man.

It was with profound relief that I found myself in Piccadilly in the wholesome company of my kind. I had carried myself boldly enough in the last hour, but I would not have gone through it again for a king's ransom. Do you know what it is to deal with a pure intelligence, a brain stripped of every shred of humanity? It is like being in the company of a snake.

I drove to the club and telephoned to Macgillivray, asking him to take no notice of my statement till he heard from me in the morning. Then I went to the hospital to see Chapman.

That Leader of the People was in a furious temper, and he was scarcely to be appeased by my narrative of the day's doings. Your Labour Member is the greatest of all sticklers for legality, and the outrage he had suffered that morning had grievously weakened his trust in public security. The Antioch Street business had seemed to him eminently right; if you once got mixed up in melodrama you had to expect such things. But for a Member of Parliament to be robbed in broad daylight next door to the House of Commons upset the foundations of his faith. There was little the matter with his body, and the doctor promised that he would be allowed up next day, but his soul was a mass of bruises.

It took me a lot of persuasion to get him to keep quiet. He wanted a public exposure of Lumley, a big trial, a general ferreting out of secret agents, the whole winding up with a speech in Parliament by himself on this latest outrage of Capitalism. Gloomily he listened to my injunction to silence. But he saw the reason of it, and promised to hold his tongue out of loyalty to Tommy. I knew that Pitt-Heron's secret was safe with him.

As I crossed Westminster Bridge on my way home, the night express to the Continent rumbled over the river. I wondered if Lumley was on board, or if he had taken one of the other ways of which he had spoken.

NINE

Return of the Wild Geese

I do not think I was surprised at the news I read in *The Times* next morning.

Mr Andrew Lumley had died suddenly in the night of heart failure, and the newspapers woke up to the fact that we had been entertaining a great man unawares. There was an obituary in 'leader' type of nearly two columns. He had been older than I thought – close on seventy – and *The Times* spoke of him as a man who might have done anything he pleased in public life, but had chosen to give to a small coterie of friends what was due to the country. I read of his wit and learning, his amazing connoisseurship, his social gifts, his personal charm. According to the writer, he was the finest type of cultivated amateur, a Beckford with more than a Beckford's wealth and none of his folly. Large private charities were hinted at, and a hope was expressed that some part at least of his collections might come to the nation.

The halfpenny papers said the same thing in their own way. One declared he reminded it of Atticus, another of Maecenas, another of Lord Houghton. There must have been a great run on biographical dictionaries in the various offices. Chapman's own particular rag said that, although this kind of philanthropist was a dilettante and a back-number, yet Mr Lumley was a good specimen of the class and had been a true friend to the poor. I thought Chapman would have a fit when he read this. After that he took in the *Morning Post*.

It was no business of mine to explode the myth. Indeed I couldn't even if I had wanted to, for no one would have believed me unless I produced proofs, and these proofs were not to be made public. Besides, I had an honest compunction. He had had, as he expressed it, a good run for his money, and I wanted the run to be properly rounded off.

Three days later I went to the funeral. It was a wonderful occasion. Two eminent statesmen were among the pall-bearers. Royalty was represented, and there were wreaths from learned societies and scores of notable people. It was a queer business to listen to that stately service, which was never read over stranger dust. I was thinking all the time of the vast subterranean machine which he had controlled, and which now was so much old iron. I could dimly imagine what his death meant to the hosts who had worked blindly at his discretion. He was a Napoleon who left no Marshals behind him. From the Power-House came no wreaths or newspaper tributes, but I knew that it had lost its power.

De mortuis, etc. My task was done, and it only remained to get Pitt-Heron home.

Of the three people in London besides myself who knew the story – Macgillivray, Chapman, and Felix – the two last might be trusted to be silent, and Scotland Yard is not in the habit of publishing its information. Tommy, of course, must some time or other be told; it was his right; but I knew that Tommy would never breathe a word of it. I wanted Charles to believe that his secret died with Lumley, for otherwise I don't think he would have ever come back to England.

The thing took some arranging, for we could not tell him directly about Lumley's death without giving away the fact that we knew of the connection between the two. We had to approach it by a roundabout road. I got Felix to arrange to have the news telegraphed to and inserted by special order in a Russian paper which Charles could not avoid seeing.

The device was successful. Calling at Portman Square a few days later, I learned from Ethel Pitt-Heron's glowing face that her troubles were over. That same evening a cable to me from Tommy announced the return of the wanderers.

It was the year of the Chilean Arbitration, in which I held a junior brief for the British Government, and that and the late sitting of Parliament kept me in London after the end of the term. I had had a bad reaction from the excitements of the summer, and in these days I was feeling pretty well hipped and overdone. On a hot August afternoon I met Tommy again.

The sun was shining through my Temple chambers, much as it had done when he started. So far as I remember, the West Ham brief which had aroused his contempt was still adorning my table. I was very hot and cross and fagged, for I had been engaged in the beastly job of comparing half a dozen maps of a despicable little bit of South American frontier.

Suddenly the door opened, and Tommy, lean and sunburnt, stalked in.

'Still at the old grind,' he cried, after we had shaken hands. 'Fellows like you give me a notion of the meaning of Eternity.'

'The same uneventful, sedentary life,' I replied. 'Nothing happens except that my scale of fees grows. I suppose nothing will happen till the conductor comes to take the tickets. I shall soon grow fat.'

'I notice it already, my lad. You want a bit of waking up or you'll get a liver. A little sensation would do you a pot of good.'

'And you?' I asked. 'I congratulate you on your success. I hear you have retrieved Pitt-Heron for his mourning family.' Tommy's laughing eyes grew solemn.

'I have had the time of my life,' he said. 'It was like a chapter out of the Arabian Nights with a dash of Fenimore Cooper. I feel as if I had lived years since I left England in May. While you have been sitting among your musty papers we have been riding like mosstroopers and seeing men die. Come and dine tonight and hear about our adventures. I can't tell you the full story, for I don't know it, but there is enough to curl your hair.' Then I achieved my first and last score at the expense of Tommy Deloraine.

'No,' I said, 'you will dine with me instead, and I will tell you the full story. All the papers on the subject are over there in my safe.'

John Buchan Authorised Editions

The John Buchan Story Museum is delighted to be partnered with Polygon Books in the publishing of John Buchan's works in paperback. One of the aims of the John Buchan Story is to introduce John Buchan's works to as wide a readership as possible. The Museum's Trustees are confident that, by collaborating with Polygon Books in producing these authorised editions, the works of John Buchan will indeed reach out to another generation.

Readers are invited to visit the museum, which is housed in the Chambers Institution on the High Street in Peebles. There, through audiovisual presentations and by viewing original artefacts, you can discover more about the life, work and legacy of this remarkable man and his connections with Peebles. For a preview of what's in the museum, visit our website: www.johnbuchanstory.co.uk.

The John Buchan Society, with which the museum collaborates, promotes his life and works. For further information visit their website: www.johnbuchansociety.co.uk.